LONNIE'S
WARRIOR
SWORD

Los Angeles • New York

Printed in the United States of America
First Hardcover Edition, August 2017
First Paperback Edition, August 2017
1 3 5 7 9 10 8 6 4 2
FAC-020093-17181

Library of Congress Control Number: 2016939523
Hardcover ISBN 978-1-4847-7867-8
Paperback ISBN 978-1-4847-9932-1

For more Disney Press fun, visit www.disneybooks.com
Visit DisneyDescendants.com

SUSTAINABLE FORESTRY INITIATIVE Certified Sourcing
www.sfiprogram.org
SFI-00993

THIS LABEL APPLIES TO TEXT STOCK

More new books coming soon in
the School of Secrets series...

NEXT:
CARLOS'S
SCAVENGER HUNT

TRAINING 101

The sword felt heavy in the young girl's hand. At only nine years old, she struggled to hold it up without her wrist buckling. But it was the weight of it that she loved. The power and history she knew it possessed. She felt strong holding her birthright. Brave. Bold. Like a warrior.

Like her mother.

"Can we try again?" the girl asked, breathlessly. She loved this mother-daughter bonding time they shared. Some children played catch with their parents. But not her. She and her mother sparred with swords. They had been training for over three hours, but the girl was not tired. She wanted to practice until the sun disappeared behind the high stone walls of the Imperial City. She wanted to practice until she was flawless. Until she was a warrior.

Like her mother.

"I think it's time to go inside, my little blossom," her mother replied, sheathing her own sword and turning back toward their house. They had been training in the gardens, next to a peaceful babbling brook surrounded by vibrant pink peony flowers. The majestic Imperial Palace, with its crimson walls and sloped blue roofs, glimmered in the distance.

"Wait!" the girl called out, still out of breath from the practice. Her mother turned around, pausing beneath a canopy of cherry blossoms in full bloom. For a moment, the girl thought it looked like a pink halo around her mother's head. "Five more minutes," the girl pleaded. She wasn't ready to quit for the day. She hadn't yet mastered everything she wanted to master.

Her mother smiled a kind, knowing smile, and took three steps back to her daughter. She reached out and touched her daughter's warm cheek. "I was once like you. Eager. Determined." She chuckled. "A little stubborn."

The girl smiled. She loved when her mother pointed out their similarities. Her mother was one of the greatest warriors the Imperial City had ever seen. Which was why the girl was out here every chance she could get. Practicing with the sword that her mother had won from the great and evil Shan-Yu.

She glanced down at the heavy weapon in her hand. It was long and jagged, with a thick steel handle. Unlike any sword the girl had ever seen before. And she knew that one day it would belong to her. Because it was her birthright. She just had to work hard enough to be worthy of it.

"But then," her mother continued, dropping her hand from the girl's face, "I learned the secret of being a true warrior."

"Higher jumps?" the girl guessed. "A stronger grip? Faster reflexes?"

Her mother's eyes crinkled. "None of those things, actually."

The girl was confused. If becoming a better warrior wasn't about faster reflexes, then what had she been spending all this time training for? Why had she been making herself dizzy running drills around the Imperial City? Climbing trees? Leaping hurdles? Balancing on the rails of fences? Was all her work for nothing?

"I don't understand," she told her mother.

"Being a valiant warrior is not about the strength you have here." She reached out and gently touched her daughter's growing bicep. "It's about the strength you have here." Her hand moved directly over the girl's heart.

The girl frowned, still unable to follow. "But how do I train for that?"

Her mother laughed. "Unfortunately, my little blossom, it's not something you can train for. It's something you can only learn when the right challenge presents itself."

The girl sighed, feeling discouraged. "But when will the right challenge present itself?"

Her mother's eyes lit up, like she knew a secret the girl did not. "Now, *there* is a wise question."

And then, just when the girl thought her mother might *answer* the question, she turned again and started walking slowly back home, her armor clanking softly with each step.

EN GARDE!

Hi, I'm Lonnie,
teenage daughter of Mulan.

My mom is one of the greatest warriors to ever live. Actually, both of my parents are. But not only is my mom a clever and powerful swordswoman, she also defeated the evil Shan-Yu and his army of Huns, instantly becoming a hero and a legend. That's a lot for a girl to live up to, believe me. But don't worry, I'm doing okay for myself. In fact, I was recently invited to be the captain of the R.O.A.R. team at Auradon Prep. It's the coolest sport. We battle with swords while doing all kinds of awesome flips and stunts. Becoming captain is a pretty big feat for a girl, given that a few months ago girls weren't even allowed on the team!

And now I plan to be the fiercest R.O.A.R. player in the history of the sport. I am going to be a legend, just like my mother. Okay, well, maybe not <u>exactly</u> like my mother, because let's face it, things have changed a lot around here. Obviously, I won't be heading off to fight any insurgent armies in the near future. But just like my mom did, I'm going to show those boys on the team that just because I'm a girl, it doesn't mean I can't hold my own. I'm going to prove to all of them that I'm worthy of being their captain.

I want to be the best at what I do.

And that brings me to my story. It's a pretty epic one, if you ask me. Maybe not like saving-the-world epic, but close enough.

I'm getting ahead of myself, though. I should probably start at the beginning. Because before you can fully appreciate my great warrior quest, you have to understand how it began.

And it all began with a book. A very important book . . .

TAKE A STAB AT IT

I've been studying the R.O.A.R. rule book for the past few weeks, trying to commit every page to memory. I am the team captain, after all, so I have to be an expert on all the ins and outs of the game.

Lonnie was sitting in the stands of the R.O.A.R. outdoor arena, the place where they competed in the fencing-meets-parkour sport, reading the official team rule book. She reread the page a third time, making certain she had understood it correctly.

Ever since first trying out for the R.O.A.R. team at Auradon Prep, Lonnie had had a love-hate relationship with that rule book. For starters, it was the rule book that had originally stated she wasn't allowed on the team, because she was a girl. It said, "The team will be comprised of a captain and eight men." But then again, it was the same vaguely worded sentence that had allowed Jay, Jafar's son, to eventually name her as captain of the team, because the rules didn't state anything about the *captain* not being a girl.

Now, as she stared at the open page on her lap and reread the big bold words in front of her for the fourth time, she was starting to lean back toward *disliking* the rule book again.

EACH MEMBER OF THE AURADON PREP R.O.A.R. TEAM SHALL BE INDUCTED AT A SPECIAL CEREMONY, DURING WHICH THE MEMBER SHALL PRESENT THEIR OFFICIAL SWORD, THE WEAPON WITH WHICH THEY WILL PARTICIPATE IN ALL FUTURE R.O.A.R. COMPETITIONS.

Lonnie sighed and cupped her chin in her hands. An official sword? That she'd use for all future competitions?

She knew it couldn't just be *any* sword. It had to be special. It had to be meaningful. And it had to be located fast. The induction ceremony was less than two weeks away. She was running out of time.

Just then, Lonnie heard a loud commotion and looked up to see her teammates clamoring into the arena, all dressed in their armor, ready for practice. Lonnie closed the book and placed it in her bag, vowing to work on her little problem later. Right now, she had a team to lead. She pulled her armor on over the blue-and-pink floral training outfit Evie had designed for her.

She walked to the center of the group and clapped her hands twice.

"Okay, everyone! We'll start with thirty push-ups. Go!" The team—including Lonnie—dropped to the floor. When they'd finished the push-ups, Lonnie led them in a few laps up and down the arena stairs and some basic stretching and warm-up drills, and then she paired everyone off to practice sparring. She paired herself with Jay because she liked sparring with him. He could be a little arrogant sometimes, but he was a good fighter, and he kept Lonnie on her toes. Plus, ever since they'd battled together on the Isle of the Lost and he'd gotten her on the R.O.A.R. team, he'd become one of her best friends.

Lonnie placed her helmet on her head and grabbed her practice sword, and they stood face to face, circling each other slowly.

Jay lunged first, but Lonnie had fast reflexes. She feinted left and he missed.

Then Lonnie lunged and Jay did a backflip, landing in a crouch. Lonnie advanced, trying to take advantage of his low position, but Jay spun at the last minute and Lonnie jabbed at the air.

Jay jumped to his feet, keeping his sword up in the

defensive position. It was then that Lonnie first noticed his sword. Like, really noticed it. It was a majestic weapon—long and silver with a gold inlay on the top and an ornate metal handle. She cocked her head to the side to study it.

"What's wrong?" Jay asked, lowering his arm.

"Nothing," Lonnie said. "I was just admiring your sword."

Jay grinned and held his sword out for her to look closely. "Well, yes, it *is* a girl magnet. Kinda like me."

Lonnie rolled her eyes and stepped forward to examine it closer. "Is this the sword you were inducted into the team with?"

"Yup," Jay said proudly. "And it hasn't steered me wrong yet. I've won every competition I've entered with this sword. The sword you're inducted with is really important."

Don't remind me, Lonnie thought, already feeling stressed out again.

"Where'd you get it?" she asked.

Jay withdrew the weapon, planted the tip into the ground, and leaned on it. "From a shop in downtown Auradon."

"You bought it?" Lonnie asked, her mind already starting to turn.

Is that what she should do? Just pick out a sword from a shop and get it over with? It would certainly be easier. And it would allow her more time to study for finals, which were coming up next week. But something about that solution made her feel hollow. Like she was missing something.

"Yeah," Jay replied. "Most people on the team inherit their swords from their parents. But obviously that wasn't an option for me."

When Lonnie looked at Jay again, she could swear she saw a flash of sadness pass over his face, but it was gone just as quickly as it had come. Then he picked up his sword again and began practicing his lunges, thrusting the sword forward and pulling it back.

"Their parents?" Lonnie repeated curiously. She glanced around the arena at her other teammates. They were all still sparring with their partners. Her eyes zeroed in on Chad Charming, the son of Cinderella and Prince Charming. His sword definitely looked like it had been made for royalty.

"Besides," Jay was saying as he continued to stab the air, "my dad wasn't really a sword kinda guy. He was more into evil snake staffs."

But Lonnie had stopped listening. She was too wrapped up in her own excited thoughts to hear anything that Jay was saying.

Of course! It's so obvious! How could I have not thought of it before?

"Lonnie?" she heard Jay say. "Hello? Are you okay?"

Lonnie blinked and brought her attention back to the arena. "Um," she said, her thoughts racing. "You know what? I just remembered I have something really important to do. Can you take over practice?"

Jay shrugged. "Sure. But where are you—"

Jay never got a chance to finish his question. Because Lonnie was already halfway up the arena steps, running like the Hun army itself was chasing her.

GET A GRIP

I can almost feel the sword in my hand. I want it so badly. I know what I have to do.

Lonnie bit her lip and gripped the pen tighter. She leaned over her desk and began writing on a crisp white sheet of paper. She knew e-mail would be much faster, but she also knew that the council preferred letters. Handwritten letters. They were ancient and old-fashioned like that.

Dear Imperial Council,
I humbly request that the sword of Shan-Yu be released to me, as it is my birthright.

The sword had been given to her mother as a gift by the Emperor after she'd defeated Shan-Yu and his insurgent army. But after the kingdom of Auradon was united and all the villains were shipped off to the Isle of the Lost, the people of Auradon were asked to relinquish their weapons, since there really was no more use for them. Most people chose to place their weapons in the Museum of Cultural History. But Lonnie's mother had chosen to place her sword in the Hall of Wisdom in the Imperial City, Lonnie's hometown. There it could be watched over by the Imperial Council, who oversaw all official matters in the Imperial City, until Lonnie was old enough to inherit it. For the time being, it was kept in a glass case in the Hall of Wisdom, where citizens and visitors to the Imperial City could visit the weapon and pay homage to all that it represented.

Lonnie could remember going to the Hall of Wisdom to look at the sword when she was a little girl. She would place her palms against the glass case in which it lay and dream of the day when the mighty weapon, soaked in so much history and importance, would belong to her. Forever.

Now that time had come. Lonnie was certain of it. She was definitely old enough. And she was definitely worthy of it. She'd fought pirates on the Isle of the Lost and helped keep Auradon safe from evil. Plus, her sword skills were so strong, she'd become captain of the R.O.A.R. team. If there had ever been a moment she felt worthy of her birthright, it was now.

Lonnie made sure to put all of this into her letter, reminding the council of her feats as an AK (Auradon kid) and her great contributions to the kingdom. When she was finished, she reread the letter five times, verifying that every word was spelled correctly and every period was in the right place.

Then she signed her name at the bottom and folded up the letter. As she did, Lonnie imagined everything that would happen after this moment. She imagined receiving the council's response, their glowing words about how brave and valiant she'd been. She imagined walking into the R.O.A.R. induction ceremony in less than two weeks with the famous and iconic sword of Shan-Yu. She fantasized about the reactions of her teammates. The dropped jaws. The wide eyes. The oohs and aahs. Of course, everyone would want to touch it. Everyone would want to hold the legendary weapon in their hands.

And then, finally, she imagined her very first R.O.A.R. competition. The shock on her opponent's face as he gazed upon her powerful sword. She could almost taste her first victory. With her warrior skills and that sword, she would be practically unbeatable.

Later, as Lonnie handed the envelope to the Royal Post messenger, she was confident the council would grant her request.

Now, all she had to do was wait.

CUT TO THE CHASE

It's been three days, and I still haven't received a response from the Imperial Council. I'm going crazy with anticipation!

Lonnie was out of her R.O.A.R. uniform and back in her traditional blue-and-pink dress, fidgeting in her usual chair in the Mad for Tea tea shop while her friends chatted nervously about their upcoming exams.

"Chemistry is going to be super hard this semester," Evie, Evil Queen's daughter, said as she grabbed a tea cake from the platter on the table. She wore a fitted blue dress, her dark hair flowing around her shoulders. "Doug and I have been quizzing each other nonstop for weeks, and I still don't have all the fairy compounds memorized."

"Don't get me started on memorizing," Jordan, the Genie's daughter, said with a groan. She was wearing blue harem pants and a gold jacket. Her fuchsia-striped hair was pulled into a tight ponytail atop her head. "Do you know how many tiny little cities we have to learn for Auradon geography class?"

"Well, if I don't pass mathematics, my mother is going to be furious," Jane said, anxiously smoothing down her ruffled frock. Jane was the daughter of the headmistress, Fairy Godmother, so the pressures on her to do well at school were higher than for most of the students.

"You'll be fine," Mal, Maleficent's daughter, assured her as she stirred her tea. Mal was looking wicked as always in purple leather and matching purple hair. "Meanwhile, I'm convinced botany class is going to kill me. Do you realize how many different types of magical plants there are?"

Normally, Lonnie would have participated in the conversation. She was just as nervous as any of them about her exams, but right now she had bigger things to worry about.

"I would have thought you'd be good at botany," Audrey, Princess Aurora's daughter, said dismissively. "After all, your mother almost killed my father with a forest of thorns."

"That's true," Mal agreed, "but do you know how many *types* of thorns there are?"

"No," Audrey replied. "And I don't want to know. I don't have any room in my brain for this. I have to cram two centuries of Auradon history in there before next Monday!"

"Isn't Auradon only, like, twenty years old?" Evie asked, looking confused.

Audrey seemed pleased to impart her knowledge. "Technically, yes. King Beast only joined the kingdoms two decades ago. *However*, the separate kingdoms that make up the United States of Auradon are extremely old. You see, back in—"

"Ugh," Freddie, Dr. Facilier's daughter, said, flicking the green feather attached to her red pinstriped dress. "Enough talk of kingdoms. Boring! Someone has got to help me study for my Remedial Goodness 101 final. I think I'm going to fail."

"And whose fault is *that*?" chirped Audrey.

Thankfully, before Audrey and Freddie could start arguing, Ally, Alice in Wonderland's daughter, stepped in, holding up a teapot and asking in her chipper British accent, "More tea, anyone?"

Everyone raised their hands. Ally walked around the room, refilling cups. Her family owned the tea shop, so she was an excellent hostess for these regular tea parties.

"Let's talk about something else," Ally suggested with a toss of her long blond hair. "Lonnie? How are your R.O.A.R. practices going?"

At first, Lonnie didn't hear the question, because she was too distracted by her own thoughts. Why hadn't the council replied to her letter yet? Had they even received it? Had the messenger delivered it to the wrong address? What if it had fallen off the delivery truck and was lying in a ditch somewhere?

"Lonnie?" asked Ally again.

That's when Lonnie realized that everyone—Mal, Evie, Jane, Freddie, Jordan, Audrey, and Ally—was staring at her, waiting for her to answer. Lonnie blinked and tried to focus back on her friends. "I'm sorry. What?"

Ally chuckled. "I was asking about the R.O.A.R. team."

Lonnie nodded absently. "Oh. Right. Sorry."

She hadn't yet told any of her friends about her request for the sword. Well, technically, that wasn't true. She'd told Jay, because she had to tell *someone*. But no one else, because she wanted it to be a surprise. They were all going to be at the big induction ceremony—the whole school was—and she wanted to see the looks on all her friends' faces when she unsheathed the famous Shan-Yu sword.

"So?" Ally said, pouring more tea into Lonnie's cup. "How are practices going?"

Lonnie could tell the girls were waiting for more detail, because they were all still staring at her, but she didn't know what to say. She couldn't exactly tell them that she'd spent the last three practices in a daze, watching the door and waiting for a messenger to show up with a letter from the council.

"They're fine. Everything is fine," she said, hoping to avoid any more questions.

"Well, you just *have* to let me do your makeup for the induction ceremony," Jordan said, leaning back in her chair and crossing her legs. "We'll do a whole new look for you.

I'll film it and put it in the Style Bazaar section of my web show! We'll call the look 'Warrior Wow'!"

Lonnie instinctively shook her head. Jordan was always trying to do Lonnie's makeup, but Lonnie wasn't super into makeup. She was all for trying out new hairstyles and clothes, but she liked to keep her makeup natural and low-key.

"Thanks, Jordan, but I think I'll stick to my regular look."

Jordan slouched in her chair, disappointed. "But just think how fierce you'd look with a little cat-eye action!"

Lonnie was about to politely decline again when the little bell above the tea shop door jingled and in walked a Royal Post messenger. "Special delivery for Miss Lonnie from the Imperial Palace."

"Oh!" Lonnie jumped out of her seat, spilling her tea all over the various plates of food on the table. "That's me!" she cried, reaching for the envelope in the messenger's outstretched hand.

She immediately knew it was the response she was waiting for. The envelope was a deep red color with the Imperial Council's official gold seal in the top left corner. She could feel her hands shaking as soon as the letter was in her grasp.

This was it! She was finally getting her birthright! The sword of Shan-Yu would soon be hers!

She almost ripped it open right then and there, but she soon remembered where she was, and she glanced around to see her friends all watching her in confusion.

"What's that?" Mal asked, tilting her head to try to read the gold seal on the front.

Lonnie quickly tucked the envelope under her arm. "Nothing. Um . . . just some . . . just a letter from my mom. I'm going to read it outside."

She quickly darted for the door, barely even noticing Ally, who was now cleaning up the mess of spilled tea.

"Don't worry," Ally grumbled as Lonnie disappeared out the door. "I'll get this."

The moment Lonnie was alone outside, she wasted no time tearing open the envelope and pulling out its contents. Like all communication from the Imperial Council, the letter was beautifully written in thick black ink on silky cream paper.

Lonnie's eyes hungrily devoured the words.

Thank you for your request to release the sword of Shan-Yu from the Hall of Wisdom. While the Imperial Council is impressed by your bravery and valiant efforts defeating villains on the Isle of the Lost, we do not believe you have yet proved your worthiness of the ancient relic. Therefore, we regret to inform you that we are denying your request for the sword.

THE PEN IS SHARPER . . .

It's true what they say. Reading those words cut me to the core.

Lonnie stood motionless outside the Mad for Tea tea shop, staring at the letter in her hand.

This has to be a joke, she thought. *The guys on the team are pranking me.*

She figured Jay must have told everyone that she was waiting on this letter, and now they were tricking her. It was probably some kind of R.O.A.R. induction ritual.

The Imperial Council couldn't possibly be turning her down.

But then again, what if it *wasn't* a joke? What if they really *were* turning her down?

Lonnie reread the letter.

. . . we do not believe you have yet proved your worthiness of the ancient relic.

Lonnie's shock quickly turned into anger.

They were saying she wasn't *worthy* of the sword? That she didn't deserve it? That she hadn't earned it? Lonnie felt her teeth gritting as her grip around the letter tightened. There had to be something she could do. Maybe she should ask her mom or dad to talk to the council. Her parents were, after all, legends in the Imperial City. If her mom appealed to the council, they'd have to listen to her, wouldn't they?

No. Lonnie immediately ruled out the idea. Her mother had earned that sword on her own. She hadn't run to *her* parents for help. She had done it herself. And so would Lonnie.

A second later, Lonnie felt a slap on her back and turned to see Jay next to her. She started and quickly folded up the letter, attempting to stuff it into her pocket. But it was too late. Jay had already seen it. He'd evidently recognized the deep red color of the envelope and the gold seal.

"No way! Is this it?" he asked, swiping the letter right out of Lonnie's hand. "What'd they say? When do you get the sword? Did they mention anything about me?"

Lonnie tried to snatch the letter back, but Jay's reflexes were even better than hers. Every time she reached for it, he expertly moved his hand out of the way.

"What?" he bellowed after he finished reading. "They said no? That's not fair! They can't do that!" He crumpled up the letter and tossed it on the ground.

Lonnie sighed and bent down to pick it up. "Unfortunately, they can."

"But the sword belongs to you!" Jay argued. "Your mother defeated a whole army to get it."

Lonnie uncrumpled the paper and smoothed out the wrinkles against her leg. "Well, technically, right now, the sword belongs to the Hall of Wisdom. Only the council can decide whether or not I'm worthy of it." Lonnie's head dropped in defeat. "And apparently I'm not."

This seemed to get Jay even more riled up. His fists balled up at his sides. "Well, that's a bunch of camel crud! Of course you're worthy of it. You're one of the best swordswomen in all of Auradon!"

Lonnie shrugged. "I guess the Imperial Council doesn't think so."

"Who is this Imperial Council anyway?"

"They're a group of eight men and women who oversee all the official matters in the Imperial City."

Jay snorted. "Well, they're stupid."

"Actually, they're not," Lonnie said with another sigh. "That's the problem. They happen to be very wise. They report directly to the All-Knowing One, one of the wisest people in all of Auradon."

"Maybe we can *steal* the sword," Jay suggested. "Security is never that great in Auradon. And I happen to be a professional."

This nearly made Lonnie laugh. "Jay, the answer to everything is not *stealing*. Besides, the Hall of Wisdom is guarded with an ancient magic. Even if we could find a way to get to the Imperial City, there's no way we could—"

"Imperial City," Jay interrupted, seemingly lost in thought. "Why does that sound so familiar?"

"Maybe because it's where my parents live. Mulan and Shang. They happen to be pretty famous."

Jay rubbed his chin pensively. "No, that's not it."

Lonnie finished smoothing the letter. She carefully refolded it and returned it to the red envelope. But just as she did, Jay grabbed it from her hand again. "Let me see that." He roughly unfolded the letter and looked at the insignia on the top of the paper.

It was a picture of the famous pagoda tower in the center of the Imperial City.

"That's it!" Jay exclaimed, his eyes sparkling like stolen jewels.

Lonnie glanced over his shoulder, trying to figure out what was getting him so worked up. "*What's* it?"

"The Auradon Warrior Challenge!"

"Huh?"

Jay slapped his knee. "The Imperial City. That's why I know it. It's where they host the annual Auradon Warrior Challenge. The one on TV."

"The show with the obstacle course?" Lonnie asked, still unsure of why Jay was bringing this up.

Jay scoffed. "It is *so* much more than just an obstacle course, Lonnie. It's the ultimate battle of strength, stamina, and willpower. Carlos and I used to watch it on TV every year when we lived on the isle, and we dreamed of being able to compete in it someday." Jay stopped and stifled a laugh with his hand. "Okay, well, *I* dreamed of being able to compete in it some day. Carlos just liked watching people fall."

Lonnie flashed a polite smile and carefully removed the letter from Jay's grasp again. "Okay, well, yeah. I guess the Imperial City is known for that too."

"Wait a minute!" Jay said, getting excited again. "Isn't the Auradon Warrior Challenge . . ." He trailed off mid-sentence and pulled his phone out of his pocket, tapping furiously on the screen. "*It is!* Yes! This is perfect! This will solve everything!" He punched the air with his fists.

Lonnie gaped at him. "What are you talking about?"

"The competition! It only happens once a year!"

Lonnie's brow furrowed. "Yes, and . . . ?"

"And . . ." Jay turned his phone around so Lonnie could see the screen. "It's *next* weekend!"

Lonnie rolled her eyes and returned the letter to the envelope again. "Fine. Go. Compete in the Auradon Warrior Whatever. Fulfill your childhood dreams. Meanwhile, I have to find another sword for the induction ceremony." She started to walk away, but Jay grabbed her by the elbow and pulled her back.

"No, no, no," he said with a laugh. "Don't you get it?"

Lonnie gave him a blank look. "Get what?"

"The Auradon Warrior Challenge is not for me. It's for *you*."

"Excuse me?"

Jay pointed at something on the screen of his phone. He was on the challenge's official website. Lonnie leaned in to read what it said:

Prove your worthiness in the most epic competition ever created!

Lonnie peered from the screen to Jay, who was looking extremely proud of himself. "You're joking, right?" Lonnie asked.

"I wouldn't joke about the AWC." Jay's expression turned serious. "You win this, and that council will have no choice but to give you the sword."

ON THE FENCE

*Jay is crazy. I couldn't possibly compete
in a televised competition.
Could I?*

Later that night, as Lonnie was eating dessert in the banquet hall after dinner, she couldn't stop thinking about her conversation with Jay. He wanted her to compete in the Auradon Warrior Challenge? She'd seen the show on TV a few times. It was broadcast all over Auradon, and apparently also on the Isle of the Lost. It was highly entertaining. Grown men and women climbing trembling walls, balancing on planks, and jumping over giant moving boulders.

Lonnie had to admit that winning the challenge would certainly get the council's attention. There was no way they could say she wasn't worthy if she won! The problem was, no one Lonnie's age had ever won the competition.

"I'll train you!" Jay had offered when she'd told him her concerns. "It'll be fun!"

"The competition is in a week," Lonnie had argued. "There's no way I'll be ready in time."

"With me as your trainer, you will," Jay had said. "I've seen every episode of that show at least five times. I know how the producers think. I know what kind of challenges there will be."

Lonnie had always admired Jay's confidence, but sometimes—like right at that moment—she thought he could be a little *over*confident.

"What about finals?" Lonnie had asked. "The competition is the same weekend as the Study Lock-In, which means we're supposed to be *studying.*"

Jay had waved this away as though studying were the last thing on his mind. And apparently it was. "We'll study extra hard this week. Besides, you're one of the smartest girls in the school. I'm sure you'll do fine."

Lonnie had opened her mouth to argue again, but Jay had instantly interrupted. "C'mon. It doesn't hurt to try. What are you afraid of?"

"Nothing!" Lonnie had replied swiftly. But it must have been *too* swiftly, because Jay had given her a strange look.

"You *are*," Jay had said, pointing at her. "You're afraid of something. The Great and Powerful Lonnie is sca—"

"No, I'm not," Lonnie had cut him off. "Just forget it." And then, Lonnie had walked away.

But now, as she finished her dessert, she wondered if Jay had been right. *Was* she afraid of something?

"Lonnie, are you okay?" someone asked, interrupting her thoughts.

It was Evie. She and Mal were staring at Lonnie from across the table in the banquet hall.

"Of course I'm okay," Lonnie said, grabbing the salt from the center of the table and sprinkling it over her bowl.

"Really?" Mal asked doubtfully. "Because you just put salt on your ice cream."

"A *lot* of salt," Evie added.

Lonnie looked down to see that her friends were right. Her strawberry ice cream was covered in tiny white crystals. She sighed. "Have you guys ever wanted something *so* badly, but it felt, um, like . . . impossible?"

Evie and Mal shared a look, and then both said at once, "Yes."

Lonnie was taken aback by their definitive answer. "You have?"

Mal nodded. "Did you forget? We're from the Isle of the Lost. A place that no one ever leaves. At least that's what we were told growing up, and yet . . ."

"Here we are!" Evie finished the thought, giving her dark hair a toss.

Lonnie bit her lip, thinking about that. It was true. Until Mal, Evie, Carlos, and Jay had been admitted to Auradon Prep by King Ben, she never in a million years thought she'd meet VKs (villain kids) in person, let alone become friends with them.

"And now," Mal went on, "Ben is working on bringing even more VKs to Auradon Prep. Dizzy, Drizella's daughter, is enrolling next semester, and if all goes well, more students will be enrolled soon."

"So you see," Evie said, "even the things that *seem* impossible oftentimes aren't."

"Exactly," Mal said. "But why are *we* telling *you* this? You're the ra-ra-go-get-'em-let's-invade-the-Isle-of-the-Lost girl. If anyone knows anything about taking chances, it's you."

Lonnie perked up when she heard this. Mal was right. She *was* that girl. She'd never let anyone tell her no or "You can't" or "Only boys allowed." That was something she'd learned from her mom. You want something, you go after it. You don't let anything stand in your way. Especially not an excuse like "It's never been done before." If her mom had listened to *that* advice, there would be no sword to begin with!

Lonnie stood up with sudden determination. "You know what? You're right. Excuse me, I have something I need to do." She started to leave, but then remembered the bowl of strawberry ice cream in front of her. "Oh, hey, do either of you guys want my dessert?"

Mal and Evie both glanced at the salted ice cream and grimaced.

"Uh, that's okay," Evie said. "But thanks!"

Lonnie shrugged and set off to find Jay.

STRONG COMPETITOR

The Auradon Warrior Challenge is
in exactly one week, so Jay and I
have to spend every waking moment
either training for the competition
or cramming for finals.

Being such an avid fan of the show, Jay was familiar with the way the AWC competition was set up. Day one was the elimination round where the competitors had to take on an obstacle course consisting of three extremely difficult challenges. The ten people who completed this obstacle course with the fastest times got to stay on and compete in the final competition on day two, which Jay said was always a big surprise, so it was virtually impossible to train for it.

"But," Jay said on their first day of training as they stood before a giant rocky cliff near the Enchanted Lake, "we *can* train for the elimination round. Now, I've watched a ton of reruns over the years, so I know this show backward and forward. They always use the elimination round to test for strength, balance, and power. Which means there's usually a swinging component, a climbing component, and a balancing component." He pointed to the top of the cliff. "We'll start with climbing."

Lonnie glanced upward and snorted. "You're kidding, right? You want me to just climb that?"

Jay shook his head. "Of course not."

Lonnie sighed in relief.

"I want you to climb that wearing these ten-pound weights." Jay opened his bag and took out two giant metal disks, which he began to strap around Lonnie's waist.

"What?" Lonnie asked. "You're crazy! That's twenty extra pounds!"

"Exactly," Jay said. "*Extra* pounds. So if you get used to climbing with these weights on, when you get to the competition and have to climb something without the weights, it'll be easy. It'll feel like you're flying!"

Jay finished securing the giant disks to Lonnie's waist and let go. Lonnie nearly toppled to the ground from the weight. She felt like an elephant. "This is impossible," she whined.

Jay leaned back and crossed his arms. "You're right. What was I thinking? You're just a girl. Girls can't do this.

It's too hard. Now, maybe if you were a guy, this would be different, but—"

Before Jay could finish, Lonnie was already three steps up the rocky cliff. There was nothing that motivated Lonnie more than being told she *couldn't* do something. Lonnie was determined to be a barrier breaker, just like her mother.

"Slow down!" Jay called after her. "You'll burn out if you go that fast."

"Don't tell me what to do!" Lonnie yelled down. "I don't take orders from you!"

She continued to climb up the rocky wall with the speed of a sprinter off the starting block. But within a few minutes, Lonnie realized that Jay was right. She was getting really tired. And before she could even get halfway to the top, she'd burned out. It was those weights. They were killing her! She finally gave up and climbed back down. When she landed beside Jay, he was smirking. He'd clearly manipulated her with that whole "Girls can't do this" remark.

"Lesson number one," he said smugly. "Never act out of emotion. Act out of confidence. It's much more reliable."

Lonnie grunted, even though she knew he was right. "Is that your philosophy for flirting with girls?"

Jay grinned. "You know it!" He turned serious again. "Your first mistake was letting me upset you and using *that* as your fuel. And lesson number two: sometimes speed is your enemy. Yes, the obstacle course is always about the top times, but you won't qualify at all if you fall off or burn out. Know when to take it slow."

Lonnie nodded, fighting to catch her breath. Jay was good. Really good. She was grateful he had agreed to train her. And at that moment, she vowed to do whatever he said, certain that if she had any chance of winning this thing, it would be with Jay's help.

In the days leading up to the competition, Lonnie spent long hours climbing trees in the forest, swinging from branches, shimmying between buildings, walking barefoot across hot coals, dodging dragon cannons on the tourney field, and balancing on spinning logs.

All the while, Jay and Lonnie brainstormed ideas for how to sneak out of Auradon Prep during the Study Lock-In weekend without anyone noticing *and* get all the way to the Imperial City, which was clear on the other side of Auradon.

By the end of the week, they were fresh out of options. They'd gone through every possible scenario they could think of and were quickly running out of time. All competitors for this year's Auradon Warrior Challenge were supposed to be in the Imperial City for the elimination round the next morning, and Lonnie still had no way to get there. They couldn't drive, because neither one of them had access to a car (and Lonnie had promptly rejected Jay's suggestion that he steal one). There was a high-speed Royal Express train, but neither of them could afford the ridiculously expensive tickets. And a boat would take far too long.

By Friday night, Lonnie was starting to lose hope of ever getting to the Imperial City.

"Do you think we should just give up?" Lonnie asked as they sat in the middle of the R.O.A.R. arena after an especially grueling day of training. "I mean, I *do* have a lot more studying to do."

"No way!" Jay said, jumping to his feet. "We've come this far. We can't give up. Besides, you've been doing so well. I really think you have a chance at winning this thing!"

Lonnie sighed. "I know. But I can't win if I can't get there!"

Jay started to pace, clearly lost in thought. "If only we could magically *poof* our way to the Imperial City."

Lonnie's head immediately shot up. "Did you say *poof*?"

Jay stopped pacing. "Yes. I realize it's a very un-VK thing to say. Please don't tell the other guys on the team."

But Lonnie wasn't thinking about the word itself. She was thinking about the *idea* that the word had just inspired.

Would it work? she thought, her heart pounding wildly. *Could I really convince her to do it?*

"Lonnie," Jay said, plopping back down beside her. He

cocked an eyebrow. "What are you thinking? Are you going to ask Mal to use her spell book? Because I'm pretty sure they put that thing in the museum."

Lonnie shook her head. "No."

"Jane, then? Because to be honest, she's still new at the whole magic thing, and I'm not sure I'd really trust her to—"

"Not Jane."

Jay threw up his hands. "Then who?"

"Are you forgetting?" A sly smile spread across Lonnie's face. "Mal and Jane aren't the only ones at Auradon Prep who can do magic."

SWORDS WITH FRIENDS

I have a new plan for getting to the Imperial City. It just requires a little . . . poof.

As she headed toward the study room on the first floor of the dorm, Lonnie started to hear a strange noise. It sounded like someone chanting something. Lonnie crept closer to the room at the end of the hall. The door was closed, which was strange, as the study room was a common area and was usually open. It was also where she could usually find the person she was looking for.

Lonnie froze when she saw puffs of pink smoke slithering out from under the closed door, and she jumped back in surprise.

What is going on in there? Lonnie wondered.

Then, a moment later, Lonnie heard a gruff voice say, "Forget it, you piece of tin!" followed by a loud *thump*, as though someone had thrown something hard against the wall.

Now Lonnie was even more nervous about making her request. But she knew she couldn't back down. So she gently rapped on the door and waited.

"Who is it?" someone called out in a sharp voice.

"It's Lonnie. Can I come in?"

There was a pause, and for a moment, Lonnie worried that she might not be allowed inside, but then the door swung open and Jordan stood there, looking frustrated.

"What?" Jordan asked.

Lonnie immediately noticed the unusually chaotic state of the study room, Jordan's favorite place to do homework. The furniture had all been moved around and the curtains had been drawn. Swatches of silk fabric had been strewn about and littered the floor. Lonnie scanned the room, taking in the mess, before her gaze finally landed on a small metal object near the wall. It was Jordan's genie lamp.

"What's going on in here?" Lonnie asked hesitantly.

Jordan crossed her arms and pouted. "Nothing."

Lonnie chuckled. "It's clearly not nothing. Why is your genie lamp on the floor?"

"Shhh!" Jordan said, her eyes darting suspiciously into the hallway. Then she grabbed Lonnie by the arm and pulled her into the study room, shutting the door behind them and locking it.

Once they were alone, Jordan huffed, "The darn thing is broken."

Lonnie's eyes widened as all her hopes of getting to the Imperial City sank into the pit of her stomach. She knew Jordan was hesitant to use magic in the first place, but if the lamp didn't even work, then this whole thing was pointless. "Your lamp is broken?"

"Well, no," Jordan admitted. "Not really. But it's useless. I really, really need to get out of this stupid promise I made to Ben, but it won't grant my wish."

"What promise?"

Jordan sighed. "It's no big deal. I just promised him I would produce a documentary about Mal, Evie, Jay, and Carlos so he could use it to bring more VKs to Auradon Prep."

"That sounds awesome!" Lonnie said. "That'll definitely help him convince the rest of the royal council."

Jordan shot her an uneasy look. "Yeah, well, I don't have the time. So I need to get out of it."

"Why don't you just tell Ben you don't have time?"

Jordan sighed. "Because I already said yes. And I don't want to bail on him. He's really counting on this documentary, but I'm just . . ." She glanced nervously at Lonnie out of the corner of her eye. "I'm just swamped with exams and everything."

Lonnie wasn't sure why, but she was getting a strange

vibe from Jordan. Maybe it was the chaotic state of the room, or maybe it was the way she was kind of shifting from foot to foot, as if she were standing on one of those beds of hot coals that Jay had been making Lonnie walk across all week. Lonnie almost felt like Jordan wasn't telling her the whole truth. She had a sneaking suspicion Jordan was holding something back.

"Jordan—" Lonnie began, but Jordan hastily cut her off.

"Anyway, so I was trying to wish myself free of my commitment, but this stupid lamp wouldn't grant my wish."

"I didn't know genies could grant themselves wishes."

Jordan sighed and sat down on the couch, looking defeated. "They can't. That's the problem." She gestured to the mess around the room. "I was trying to find a loophole. Spells. Incantations. Spirit dances. But nothing worked."

Lonnie sat down next to Jordan. "That *is* frustrating."

"You have no idea."

Lonnie nodded. "You're right. I don't. We don't have any magic in my family. Sometimes I wish we did, though."

"No, you don't," Jordan replied. "It just complicates things. Not to mention magic is totally frowned upon. But this is really important, so I figured it was worth the risk. But honestly, what's the point of being a powerful genie when you can't help yourself out of a tiny little problem? I mean, I can use this lamp to grant three wishes to anyone in the world . . . except myself."

Lonnie perked up, remembering the reason she'd come in here. "Wait a minute. I might have a solution."

Jordan looked over at Lonnie, seemingly intrigued. "I doubt it, but what?"

"Remember that story your father always likes to tell about Aladdin using his third wish to set your dad free?"

"Yeah," Jordan said warily. "What about it?"

"That's it!" Lonnie said, jumping up from the couch. "That's the solution."

"My dad can't grant me wishes, either," Jordan said. "And Aladdin is all the way out in—"

"Not Aladdin. Me!"

"You?"

Lonnie beamed. "Yes! I can make your wish for you. If you grant *me* three wishes, I'll use one of them on you."

Of course, she didn't even need two wishes. She only needed the one. She needed to get Jay and herself to the Imperial City during the Study Lock-In without Fairy Godmother finding out.

Jordan still looked skeptical. "Wait, what do *you* need to wish for?"

Lonnie glanced over both her shoulders to make sure she wasn't going to be overheard. Then she leaned in and asked Jordan, "Can you keep a secret?"

Jordan flashed a mischievous grin. "Of course."

Lonnie smiled back at her friend with a twinkle in her

eye. "Ever heard of the Auradon Warrior Challenge?"

"Yes," Jordan replied warily.

"Well, it's sort of a long story, but basically I need to get to the Imperial City this weekend to compete in the challenge so I can prove to the Imperial Council that I'm worthy of my mother's sword. Except I have no way of getting there."

"And you want *me* to help you get there?"

Lonnie nodded toward the lamp still lying on the floor. "You and your lamp, yes. I mean, I know you're not supposed to use magic, but I thought, I don't know, maybe you'd make this one exception. For me?"

Jordan was silent for a long time. Lonnie figured she was thinking it all through. "So if I grant you three wishes," she finally said, "and poof you over to the Imperial City, then you'll save one of your wishes for me?"

Lonnie grinned. "Absolutely. I'll set you free from your commitment to Ben." But a second later, Lonnie had a thought. "Wait a minute. If you don't have time to make the documentary, why don't you just use your wish to magically finish it?"

Jordan considered that for a moment before throwing the question back at Lonnie. "Why don't you use *your* wish to just *get* your mom's sword?"

Lonnie thought about that. She supposed if Jordan agreed to let her use the lamp, she could just *wish* to win the competition or *wish* to get the sword. But that felt like cheating. She really wanted to *earn* the sword. The same way her mother had earned the sword, and the same way Lonnie had earned her spot on the R.O.A.R. team. By proving herself. She just needed to be able to *get* there to do it.

"Because I don't want to win that way," Lonnie finally replied.

Jordan smiled. "And neither do I."

Lonnie immediately understood. It was exactly the way she felt. If Jordan used magic to make a great documentary, it wouldn't really be *hers*.

"So do we have a deal?" Lonnie asked, sticking out her hand.

Jordan shook it. "Deal." Then she got to her feet and strolled over to her backpack and began putting her belongings back into it. "*Sooooo* . . . when do we leave?"

"Oh," Lonnie said, surprised. "Are you coming?"

"Duh," Jordan said. "I can't grant you a wish and not see it through. What if something goes wrong?"

Lonnie quickly decided she liked the idea of having one of her close friends with her. It would be like a road trip . . . except they'd be poofing instead of driving. "We leave tomorrow morning. Before breakfast."

"Perfect," Jordan said, continuing to throw things in her backpack. "I've always loved that show. I used to watch it with my dad all the time."

Lonnie was about to leave to get started with her own packing when something Jordan said stopped her. She'd been worrying about it all week. Everyone seemed to watch this show. Which meant everyone would be watching it this weekend, too. And everyone she knew would recognize her.

"Jordan?" Lonnie said meekly.

Jordan looked up from her duffel bag. "Yeah?"

"I think I might need one more thing."

She laughed. "Well, you still have one more wish, so whatever you want!"

Lonnie bit her lip. "Actually, this is more of a personal *favor*."

Jordan lifted one eyebrow.

Lonnie shuffled her feet, feeling anxious about what she was going to ask. But she knew it needed to be done. Especially if she wanted any hope of getting away with this crazy plan without getting caught. She sighed and said, "Can you do my makeup for the challenge? I need a whole new look."

TIPS AND TRICKS

Jordan is the queen of the makeover. I know she's going to give me a fierce new look. I told her to think "warrior chic."

"Are you sure that's not too much eye shadow?" Lonnie asked the next morning as she sat in her dorm room with a giant makeup bag open on the bed next to her.

Jordan rolled her eyes and plunged her brush back into the tin of purple powder. "No," she said resolutely. "Now, close your eyes."

Lonnie closed her eyes and felt the tickle of the brush on her lids as Jordan applied yet another layer of pigment. "Because it feels like it might be too much."

"Do you want to be recognized by all of Auradon?" Jordan asked.

"No."

"Then let me do my job."

Lonnie sighed and allowed Jordan to finish her makeup. Jordan hadn't let Lonnie look in the mirror since they'd started. She said no one should look upon a work of art until it was finished. So Lonnie had no idea what Jordan had been doing with her face. All she knew was that it had been taking forever, and it was *way* more makeup than she'd ever worn in her life. She was starting to worry about what she would see when she did look in a mirror.

"And now for the final touch," Jordan said, digging something out of her bag. A moment later, she pulled out a blond wig and placed it on Lonnie's head, tucking in Lonnie's dark hair around the edges.

"A wig?" Lonnie asked. "Is that really necessary?"

"Yes," Jordan said. "You asked me to make you look older and different. This will do it. And if you don't want to automatically be identified as Mulan's daughter, you need to change everything about your appearance."

Lonnie sighed. "Well, just make sure it stays on. I'm a warrior. I do flips and stuff."

Jordan rolled her eyes. "I got it. I got it."

After every strand of Lonnie's long dark hair was tucked under the wig and Jordan had applied a layer of lip gloss and mascara, she finally held up a mirror for Lonnie to look at her reflection.

At first, Lonnie didn't believe what she was seeing. She was convinced Jordan had given her some kind of magic mirror. Maybe even Evie's magic mirror. Because there was no way that was *her* reflection in the glass. The girl staring back looked nothing like her! While Lonnie normally had a soft, natural look, this girl was wild and fierce, with dark painted eyes, deep purple-tinted lips, and a sleek blond bob.

It wasn't until Lonnie blinked and the girl in the mirror blinked, too, that Lonnie was actually able to convince herself it was her.

"Wow," Lonnie said, flabbergasted.

"Thank you," Jordan said, beaming. "It is pretty wicked, isn't it?"

"It's unbelievable," Lonnie said. "I look *so* much older."

"No one is ever going to recognize you."

"*I* don't even recognize me!" Lonnie said with a giggle.

"Let me take a picture," Jordan said, holding up her phone and angling it toward Lonnie's face.

"Okay, but you can't show it to anyone," Lonnie reminded her. "You're sworn to secrecy, remember?"

"Yeah, yeah, I know," Jordan said and snapped the photo.

It was then that Lonnie noticed she and Jordan had the exact same fuchsia phone case. "Hey!" Lonnie said, pulling out her own phone. "We have matching phones!"

Jordan grinned. "I'm not surprised. We both have awesome taste!"

Lonnie giggled and continued to examine her new look in the mirror. She could hardly contain her excitement. She was going to the Imperial City! To compete in the Auradon Warrior Challenge! After all her relentless training with Jay this week, she was feeling more and more confident that she might actually be able to win this thing. Jay certainly thought she had what it took. Soon enough, she'd prove to the council that she was worthy. And her mother's sword, with all its history and magnificence, would soon be hers!

"Okay," Jordan said, "so now, the important question. What are you going to wear?"

Lonnie glanced down at her outfit. "Um, this?" She was dressed in black pants, a black jacket, and a black belt with gold clasps. She couldn't wear her traditional R.O.A.R outfit, because she might be recognized in it. This felt like a good disguise.

Jordan took a step back to study Lonnie's black pants, jacket, and belt. "Hmmm. Are you sure you don't want to go with something a bit bolder?"

"I need to be comfortable," Lonnie argued. "And I'm comfortable in this."

Jordan shrugged and picked up her duffel bag. "Okay. Whatevs. Let's get this show on the road."

Lonnie put down the mirror and glanced at Jordan. She was wearing what she usually wore, but Lonnie couldn't help noticing how stylish and put together she looked. Then again, Jordan always looked good. Lonnie supposed she had to, considering Jordan was the host of one of the most famous web shows in Auradon. It was her sense of style and personality that made the web show so popular. Jordan was really skilled in the production side of things, too. She was a wiz at editing together compelling storylines and flashy montages. Which was why it was too bad she hadn't had time to produce the documentary for King Ben. Lonnie knew it would have been amazing. Jordan could probably film corn growing and make it look interesting. Lonnie had always wanted to ask Jordan to help her film a hip-hop video, but lately she'd become so preoccupied with the R.O.A.R. team, her hip-hop dancing had taken a back seat. Plus, if Jordan didn't have time to make that documentary, she definitely wouldn't have time to do a video for Lonnie.

"Are you ready?" Jordan asked. She removed her magic genie lamp from her shimmery gold purse and held it out to Lonnie. Lonnie took it, feeling kind of giddy at the weight of it in her hands.

It felt different from how she'd always imagined. Heavier, yes, but not just from the metal. It felt more significant somehow. Like all those past wishes were giving it shape and weight and a feeling of hopefulness.

"Go ahead," Jordan said. "Give it a rub and then"—she bowed—"your wish is my command."

"Actually," Lonnie said, glancing toward the door. "I'm just waiting for one more person."

"What?" Jordan's eyes grew wide. "Who?"

Then, as if in answer to Jordan's question, there was a knock on the door and in walked Jay. Actually, Jay hardly just *walked*. It was really more of a strut.

Jay was looking cool as usual in his black pants, black lace-up boots, yellow and maroon vest, and red knit hat. He had a single backpack slung casually over his shoulder.

Jay raised his hands in the air. "What's up, ladies? The party can finally begin. Jay is here." Then Jay must have noticed Lonnie's new look, because he stopped and his mouth fell open. "Lonnie? Is that you?"

Jordan let out a loud groan, which she did absolutely nothing to hide from Jay. "What is *he* doing here?"

"Nice to see you, too, my sweet genie girl," Jay said with a smug grin.

"I am *not* your genie girl," Jordan said, then flashed an accusing look at Lonnie. "You didn't tell me *he* was coming."

"Oh," Lonnie said, surprised by Jordan's reaction. "I'm sorry. I didn't think you'd mind."

"Well, I mind," Jordan snapped.

Lonnie blinked in confusion. What was that about? She

thought Jordan and Jay got along well. Or as well as the son of Jafar and the daughter of the Genie *could* get along. But now Jordan was acting like Lonnie had just announced she was bringing Jafar himself on the trip.

"Jay's my trainer. He has to come," Lonnie explained, although she still didn't know why she even *had* to explain.

Jordan crossed her arms. "I'm sorry. I'm not going if he's going."

"What?" Lonnie asked, shocked. "Why?"

Lonnie knew Jay could be a little full of himself. And she could see how that might come off as annoying to some people. But Jordan had never seemed to mind it before. In fact, they had become friends after Jay had come to Auradon Prep. Plus, ever since joining the R.O.A.R. team, Lonnie had seen a different side of him. A softer side. A friendlier side. That was the Jay she had become such good friends with.

"Because," Jordan said, still refusing to even make eye contact with Jay, "I thought this was going to be a girls' trip."

"It is," Jay said, stepping between Lonnie and Jordan and putting his arms around both of them. "Just think of me as one of the girls."

Jordan scoffed. "Yeah, right."

"C'mon," Jay said, joking with Jordan. "It could be really

romantic. You and me on a trip together. The daughter of the Genie and the son of Jafar. Star-crossed lovers. I could steal a magic carpet and fly us into the sunset. Show you a whole new world."

Jordan's nose crinkled as though she smelled something rotten. She pushed Jay away. "Ugh, no."

Jay pretended to stumble from Jordan's shove. "Whoa. You got some muscles on you, genie girl. Maybe we should be entering *you* in the competition."

"Stop calling me genie girl," Jordan said.

"Why?" Jay asked. "You're a genie . . . and you're a girl. It's an accurate description."

"Please come, Jordan," Lonnie pleaded. "I really want you there. Not only because you're my genie, but because you're my friend."

Jordan scoffed and uncrossed her arms. "Fine. Whatever. Let's just get this over with."

Lonnie sighed with relief. Maybe Jordan was just in a bad mood this morning and was taking it out on Jay. Lonnie hoped that whatever disdain Jordan had toward Jay would wear off sooner rather than later; otherwise this would be a very long weekend.

Jordan nodded toward the lamp still clutched in Lonnie's hand. "Make your wish already."

Lonnie glanced down at the golden object in her hand

and felt her heart start to hammer with anticipation. She knew that the lamp granted three wishes. She'd planned to use one to get them to the Imperial City without being caught and the other for getting Jordan out of her commitment to Ben. Which meant there was still one wish left. She decided she was going to save that one in case of an emergency.

Lonnie closed her eyes and rubbed the lamp in her hand.

"I wish for us all to go to the Imperial City," she whispered aloud, before quickly adding, "without getting caught."

Then she waited. At first, nothing happened. And Lonnie worried that she had done something wrong. Said the wrong words. Rubbed the wrong part of the lamp. Making wishes on genie lamps wasn't a subject they taught at Auradon Prep.

But a few seconds later, a strange thing started to happen. Lonnie felt the lamp tingle between her fingers. She opened her eyes to see glittery pink smoke floating out of the lamp's spout. It started as a small stream—barely even as wide as her pinky finger—but then it began to grow and puff and expand. Like it was alive and breathing. The smoke got wider and wider until it encompassed all three of them and she could no longer see Jay or Jordan.

"Uh," she heard Jay say with a cough. "Is this supposed to happen?"

"Yes," Jordan snapped. "Be quiet. I'm concentrating."

Lonnie was about to ask another question but quickly closed her mouth, partly because she didn't want to disrupt Jordan's concentration, but also because she didn't want to inhale too much of the pink smoke. For a moment, she wondered if maybe this wish was too big for Jordan. Maybe she wasn't quite skilled enough as a genie to grant it.

But then, in the blink of an eye, the smoke vanished as though it had never been there to begin with, and Lonnie glanced at her new surroundings. They were no longer standing in Lonnie's dorm room. They were standing next to a babbling brook surrounded by lush, rolling green grass and beautiful vibrant pink peony flowers. Lonnie immediately recognized it as the gardens near the Imperial Palace, where she used to train and practice with her mother when she was a little girl. She could see the sloped wooden framework of the palace peeking out over the hill and the tall buildings of the Imperial City just beyond that.

And it wasn't just the sights that were familiar. It was the smells, too. The sweet aroma of cherry blossoms in the air. The faint scent of jasmine in the breeze. The whole thing brought back so many warm and happy memories of Lonnie's childhood: sword fighting with her mother in the gardens, running laps around the palace with her father, watching the golden sun set behind the majestic pagoda that stood tall in the center of the city, baking cookies in the kitchen with her mom when she was feeling sad.

Lonnie breathed in everything and smiled a huge, blissful smile.

She was home.

ADVANCE

*I'm here! Time to go to battle!
Not the real kind, of course . . .
the reality TV kind.*

"I'll just take that," Jordan said, easing the lamp from Lonnie's grip. She then placed the lamp back in her bag and gave it a pat. "Better that I hold on to it. For safekeeping." Then she spun in a slow circle, taking in her surroundings. "So, where is this warrior festival thing?"

"It's in the center of the city," Lonnie said, pointing over the hill. "That way."

Jordan made a *tsk tsk* sound with her tongue. "See, this is why it's important to be super specific with your wishes. Otherwise you wind up in the middle of nowhere and have to walk." She gathered up her duffel bag and heaved it over her shoulder. "Geez, this thing is heavy."

"I'll carry it for you." Jay practically pushed Lonnie aside to offer his assistance to Jordan. "As you can see, I have very impressive muscles." Jay shoved up the sleeve of his shirt and began flexing his arms this way and that. Lonnie almost laughed aloud at how ridiculous he looked.

Jordan just snorted and stepped around him. "I can carry my own bag, thank you very much."

As the three of them walked toward the city, Lonnie noticed that Jay was acting very strange. He kept doing crazy jumps off garden walls or leaping up to catch high branches on trees, then backflipping off them. It almost seemed like he'd eaten too much sugar for breakfast.

"What are you doing?" Jordan asked, sounding annoyed after Jay had picked up three apples from under a tree and started to juggle them.

Jordan rolled her eyes at him. But Jay seemed determined to amuse her.

He spotted a small bridge running over a stream, and his eyes seemed to light up. He dropped the apples and leaped onto the handrail of the bridge, attempting to glide across it. Except the handrail must have been sticky or something, because his shoes skipped on the surface, and before he could stop himself, Jay went tumbling into the creek below.

Lonnie and Jordan both burst out laughing. Jay stood up and grudgingly wrung the water out of his long hair.

"I guess it's a good thing *you're* not the one entering the challenge today," Jordan commented.

Jay just scoffed in response. Meanwhile, Lonnie was wondering what all this absurd behavior was about. Why was Jay acting so foolish? She'd seen him trying to impress girls before, but never with this much eagerness.

When they finally arrived in the heart of the Imperial City, Lonnie was amazed to see how it had been transformed for the competition. There were banners strung across almost every building, welcoming the competitors; hundreds of little stands and kiosks had popped up along the street, selling souvenirs and T-shirts and good-luck charms for the challengers; and TV crews and reporters were arriving in droves, hauling equipment out of trucks and vans. Lonnie was definitely grateful for her disguise. In the center of everything, a huge red dome had been constructed: the Auradon Warrior Challenge Arena. That's where all the action would take place that day and the next.

"Um, what are you planning to do about your parents?" Jordan asked, stepping up next to Lonnie and staring at the arena. "Aren't you worried about them finding out you're here and then telling the school?"

Lonnie waved this concern away. "Nah. First of all, they live pretty far outside of town. And second, they hate reality TV, so there's no chance they'll be watching."

The three headed over to a registration table that had been set up under a tent just outside the entrance to the dome.

"Name?" a lady asked from behind a tablet.

"Um." Lonnie hesitated, trying to come up with a good fake name to give. She finally settled on her grandmother's name. "Li."

The lady typed the name into the tablet. "You'll be competitor 178," she said. "What's your helmet size?"

"Um," Lonnie said again.

"She's a small," Jay put in. Lonnie turned to him with a questioning look. "I had to order your helmet for R.O.A.R.," he explained.

The woman handed her an official Auradon Warrior Challenge helmet. It reminded Lonnie of the helmets ancient warriors used to wear to battle. It was gold, with ornate wings carved into the sides.

Lonnie fell in love with it the moment she slipped it over her blond wig. It made her feel like a real warrior. "How do I look?" she asked Jordan.

"Like someone I wouldn't want to mess with," Jordan replied.

"Perfect," Lonnie said.

"Do *not* lose your helmet," the woman said in a warning tone. "It's mandatory for the obstacle course. They won't let you on any of the equipment without a helmet. It's a legal issue." Then, in a high-pitched voice, the woman chirped, "Safety first!"

Lonnie nodded. "Got it."

"The elimination round starts in two hours. If you make it into the final round, you'll be given a royal suite in the Imperial Palace for the night."

"A suite in the palace?" Jay echoed excitedly. *"SWEET!"* He nudged Jordan. "Get it? Sweet? Suite?" He snickered at his own joke.

"I get it," Jordan deadpanned. "It's not that funny."

Jay feigned offense. "It's really funny." He turned to Lonnie. "That was funny, right?"

But Lonnie didn't want to get involved in whatever weird thing was going on between Jordan and Jay, so she stayed silent.

"Lonnie," Jay urged. "Funny, right? Suite. Sweet."

"Not that funny," the registration lady declared.

Jay snorted. "Whatever."

The registration lady turned back to Lonnie. "You can warm up in the Training Center." She pointed to a large open area that had been set up next to the dome. Then she shot a glance at Jordan and Jay. "But I'm afraid the Training Center is open to competitors and trainers only."

Jordan shrugged. "No matter. I have some shopping I want to do. I'll be in the arena to watch you crush everyone in the first round, though!" She turned and swaggered away from the table.

"I'll miss you, genie girl!" Jay called after her.

"No, you won't!" Jordan called without turning around.

"Good luck, Li!" the lady at the registration table said and then directed her attention at the next person in line.

Jay and Lonnie headed to the Training Center to warm up with the other competitors. There were several obstacles set up around the large outdoor area, and about a hundred competitors were all taking turns on them. There was an equal number of men and women, but every competitor in the room seemed older than Lonnie and looked ten times stronger and more experienced. She'd never seen so many muscles in one place before. Lonnie's whole body seemed to freeze in place.

She suddenly felt very foolish. What was she thinking, believing she could win this thing?

"This was a mistake," Lonnie whispered to Jay. She turned and tried to bolt, but Jay caught her by the arm.

"Oh, no, you don't. We didn't work this hard for you to quit before you even try."

"B-b-but," Lonnie stammered, watching a young man in blue armor and a matching blue jacket leap over a moving fence like he had springs in his boots.

"But nothing," Jay said, walking to stand in front of Lonnie so he could look into her eyes. "You are good. You can do this. Just ignore everyone else and focus on everything we've been working on."

Lonnie tried to take Jay's advice, but she couldn't keep her eyes off the guy in blue. Now he had moved on to lifting giant kettle bells over his head as though they weighed nothing.

Jay turned to follow Lonnie's fearful gaze. "Oh," he said knowingly. "Yeah, that's Chen. He's won the past four years."

"Four years?" Lonnie croaked. "You didn't tell me I was going up against a four-time champion!"

Jay waved this away as though it were an annoying fly. "I'm not worried."

"*I* am!"

"Look, would I have offered to train you if I didn't think you could win? I'm not one to associate with losers. The guy is old. He's tired. It's time for a new champion."

"How old is he?" Lonnie asked.

Jay shrugged. "Twenty-five."

Lonnie had never felt younger and less confident in her life.

Just then, Chen seemed to take notice of Lonnie and Jay standing near the entrance. He started to walk over to them, flashing a smile as he approached. But it wasn't a kind smile. It was a snakelike smile that made Lonnie squirm.

"Well, well, what do we have here?" asked Chen, giving Lonnie a once-over. "Fresh meat?"

Lonnie was speechless. Even though she'd battled nasty pirates on the Isle of the Lost, she'd never felt more intimidated than she did right at this moment.

Jay stepped in front of her. "Better than old soggy meat that's way past its expiration date."

Chen's smile fell from his face, and he shot a glare at Jay. "I don't like your tone."

Jay stood up straighter. "I don't like your face."

"Okay, okay! Enough." Lonnie stepped between them before things got out of hand. "Let's try to be civil."

Chen tore his eyes from Jay and focused back on Lonnie. "You know, we have a tradition here in the Training Center. All newbies must battle the Mountain of Doom against the reigning champ." Chen gestured toward a giant structure behind him. It was a huge climbing wall fashioned to look like the side of a rugged mountain. It was at least thirty feet tall.

Lonnie smiled, feeling *slightly* more confident. Jay had trained her for this. How many times had he made her climb that cliff near the Enchanted Lake . . . and with *weights* on? He'd said it would make her feel lighter on the day of the competition. And now, she was feeling lighter than ever.

"So what do you say?" Chen asked. "Are you up for the challenge? Or are you too scared?"

"You don't have to do this," Jay whispered in her ear. "This is just an intimidation tactic. He's trying to poke holes in your confidence so you'll mess up later. Save your energy for the elimination round."

A small crowd was starting to gather around them.

Lonnie could feel countless eyes on her. Judging her. Waiting for her to back down.

Lonnie smiled at Jay. "Don't worry. I got this." Then she turned to Chen. "You're on."

Chen grinned, like he had a secret he was keeping. He clapped his hands together, his massive muscles flexing with each slap. "Let's do this! First one to the top wins."

"Hmmm," Lonnie said, staring up at the towering wall. "Seems a little too easy."

Chen appeared to choke on something. "Excuse me?"

Lonnie shrugged. "I just think we should make things more interesting."

Chen glanced around at the growing crowd of spectators. They were starting to whisper things. Lonnie got the feeling that no one had challenged Chen before. He cleared his throat. "What did you have in mind?"

"First one to the top wins," Lonnie repeated. Her lips split into a wide grin. She had a secret, too. A secret weapon. "Except we do it with twenty-pound weights on."

A FIERCE OPPONENT

Weighted climbing? I got this. Chen has no idea what he's in for!

Lonnie and Chen took their positions at the base of the climbing wall, with giant weighted disks strapped around their waists. A fellow competitor stood nearby with a whistle, waiting to signal them.

"On your marks," he said.

Lonnie and Chen both grabbed on to the side of the wall.

"Get set."

Lonnie lifted her foot, poised and ready.

The whistle blew and they were off. Chen shot up like a rocket, finding his footing easily and quickly. Lonnie moved more slowly. She could hear Jay's voice in her head.

Lesson number two: sometimes speed is your enemy. Know when to take it slow.

While Chen scrambled up the first half of the wall, Lonnie took her time, securing her grip, digging her feet in. She knew from training with this same amount of weight that you had to conserve your energy. Twenty extra pounds was a lot to carry. It was easy to let adrenaline take over and push you to move faster. But she'd learned firsthand that it was the quickest way to burn out.

"How does it feel to look up to me?" Chen called down.

Lonnie glanced up to see that he was more than halfway to the top, at least five feet above her. She felt the urge to move faster, push herself harder, but she could hear Jay's voice in her head again.

Lesson number one: never act out of emotion. Act out of confidence. It's much more reliable.

Below her, Lonnie could hear the crowd cheering. Most of them were calling out Chen's name. She attempted to drown out the sound.

"Focus," she told herself quietly. "Do the best you can."

Lonnie took a deep breath and continued her slow yet steady pace up the wall, eventually finding a rhythm. Grip, step, pull. Grip, step, pull.

She kept her gaze trained on the wall and her thoughts trained on her task.

In fact, she was so focused and intent, she didn't even notice when she'd reached the top. That is, until she extended her arm up for her next grip and felt nothing but air. She blinked out of the trance she had sunk into and looked down.

The ground seemed so far below her now. But she could see everyone jumping up and down and clapping—Jay more so than anyone. She glanced around for Chen, certain he must have reached the top a while ago. And that's when her eyes landed on something blue a few feet below her. It was Chen's armor.

He peered up at the top of the wall, and Lonnie could see how red his face was, how ragged his breathing was. He'd gone too fast. He wasn't used to the extra weight, and he'd burned out.

Chen sneered up at her, and Lonnie repeated his earlier words with a bright smile. "How does it feel to look up to me?" she asked.

Chen let out a grunt and started to climb down. Once he was close enough to the ground, he jumped, landing in a crouch. The crowd was still cheering, except now they were chanting, "Li! Li! Li!" Chen pushed his way through them and stormed off.

Lonnie made her way back to the ground, where she was met by more raucous applause and a congratulatory pat on the back by Jay. "Well done, Captain."

Lonnie beamed. "I couldn't have done it without you."

Jay playfully bumped her shoulder. "Yeah, yeah, we make a good team. But let's not forget where the real challenge is. You may have knocked Chen off his game, but you still have to beat him out *there*." Jay pointed toward the colossal red dome that loomed just outside of the Training Center. "Don't get too full of yourself."

Lonnie guffawed. "Look who's talking!"

Jay rolled his eyes. "You know what I mean. Just because you outsmarted him here with the whole extra weight thing doesn't mean—"

"Wow!" one of the female competitors said, patting Lonnie on the back. "That was amazing! No one has ever beaten Chen on the Mountain of Doom. You might actually have a chance at winning this whole thing!"

Lonnie's grin grew wider. "You were saying?" she asked Jay.

Jay shook his head. "I'm just trying to tell you, Chen is a strong competitor. Don't underestimate him. Plus, he's desperate to prove something. No one has ever won five years in a row. He'd be the first, and he's not going to easily give up the chance to make history."

Lonnie reached out and ruffled Jay's hair. "You worry too much, you know? That sword is as good as mine."

FIGHT IT OUT

My mom always told me to believe in myself. I'm definitely going to need to channel her courage today!

As soon as Lonnie entered the Auradon Warrior Challenge arena, she felt almost all her former confidence disappear. There were *so* many people. Thousands and thousands of spectators were packed into the stands. And that wasn't even counting all the TV crew and producers. Lonnie felt as though her stomach had dropped to her knees.

Was she really ready for all of this?

Climbing a wall in the small Training Center was one thing. But performing in front of all these people, not to mention all the people watching on TV across the entire kingdom? That was something else entirely. She suddenly wasn't sure she was ready.

"You're ready," Jay said, walking beside her and giving

her shoulder a reassuring pat. It was as though he could read her mind. Or more likely, he could just read the terror in her eyes as she gazed up at the stands. She tried to wipe the fear from her face. She didn't want anyone to see how nervous she was.

Lonnie reached up and checked the position of her wig, making sure it was on straight. She couldn't very well risk all of Auradon finding out her true identity as the daughter of the legendary warrior Mulan.

In the center of the arena, the famous AWC obstacle course had been set up, but it was currently covered by a giant white sheet that shielded the various elements from view. In a few minutes, the course would be unveiled to the competitors . . . and all the viewers at home. Lonnie itched to peer under that sheet and see what she was up against.

Ari, the well-known host of the show, was standing in the center of the arena next to the concealed course, speaking to the giant crowd with a microphone that made his voice echo across the whole arena.

"Welcome to the annual Auradon Warrior Challenge! Our elimination round is about to begin! Only ten of our competitors will move on to the final competition tomorrow morning. Those who complete today's course with the fastest times will qualify for the finals. The rest of them will be going home tonight."

The crowd cheered loudly, loving the drama and suspense.

Lonnie felt a lump form in her stomach. She glanced anxiously around at her fellow competitors, trying to size them up with just a look. Her gaze landed on Chen, and he glared back at her. He was clearly *not* happy about being humiliated in front of everyone back in the Training Center, and he'd been shooting Lonnie dirty looks ever since.

Lonnie searched the crowd, trying to find Jordan in the stands. She was easy to spot with that fuchsia-streaked hair and gold jacket. Plus, she was sitting in the front row, cheering loudly. She caught Jordan's eye, and Jordan gave her an encouraging smile that immediately made Lonnie feel better.

But it didn't last long. Because as soon as she glanced back at the covered obstacle course, another bolt of panic shot through her.

What if they reveal something I can't do? Something I haven't prepared for? What if I fail miserably in front of all of these people? Not to mention everyone watching on TV?

Her heart hammered in her chest at the thought.

"Don't worry," Jay whispered. "You got this."

She tried to muster a smile for him, but it was hard with all these nerves.

"Are you ready to see what our brave warriors will be battling today?" Ari yelled to the crowd.

The stands erupted in boisterous applause and shouts. Fists were pumped in the air and whoops of excitement echoed throughout the massive red dome. Lonnie took a deep breath, trying to psych herself up. She was ready. She could do this.

"Unveil the course!" the host commanded, and a second later, the giant white sheet floated gracefully up into the air, revealing the three obstacles underneath.

Lonnie inhaled sharply as her eyes scanned the course.

"The first challenge," Ari announced dramatically, "is called the Monkey's Dare."

Lonnie turned her gaze on the element closest to her. There was a giant river dug into the ground, and hanging high above it were eight dangling ropes.

"The warrior must make it across the water using only the ropes."

While some of her fellow competitors gasped at the difficulty of the task, Lonnie breathed a sigh of relief. She could do that! It was just like when Jay had made her swing from tree branches for hours on end, timing how long she could go without falling or letting go. He'd said it was designed to strengthen her grip and her ability to propel herself using only her body weight. She'd hated that exercise, and she'd always wanted to skip it.

Jay smirked next to her. "Aren't you glad I made you swing from all those branches?"

Lonnie let out a nervous laugh. "I never thought I'd say this, but *yeah!*"

"The second challenge," the host proclaimed, "is called the Great Wall of Fire!"

Lonnie turned her attention to the middle of the arena, where two giant brick walls had been constructed over another body of water. The distance between the walls appeared to be about the length of a person.

"Each warrior must shimmy between the two walls with their feet on one wall and their hands on the other."

"Ooh!" chorused the crowd with excitement.

Meanwhile, more shocked gasps permeated the group of competitors, but Lonnie was growing more confident by the second. Jay had prepared her for this, too! She'd been practicing this very thing between Auradon Prep buildings for the past week!

"Oh, and one more thing," Ari added with a dark laugh. "The walls are scalding hot. So don't forget your gloves! And don't linger!"

Lonnie gulped. Okay, Jay hadn't exactly prepared her for *that* part.

"Don't worry about it," Jay said coolly. "You'll just have to shimmy a little faster. No sweat."

"Actually," Lonnie said, "I think *sweat* is exactly what I'll be doing between those scalding hot walls."

"And finally!" the host bellowed into the microphone. "The last challenge is called the Bridge of Despair."

Lonnie swallowed and cast her eyes to the right, where

she saw another deep ravine cut into the floor of the arena. The only thing bridging the water was an impossibly narrow metal pole.

"To complete this challenge, warriors must cross the ravine using the bridge."

"Oh, you *so* got this!" Jay whispered excitedly beside her.

Lonnie exhaled a huge breath. He was right. She *did* have this. This was going to be a breeze! Jay had made her practice this very skill with logs at the Enchanted Lake. Except in Jay's version, it was even harder, because the logs were spinning.

"Oh, I nearly forgot," the host said with a practiced smirk. He signaled a technician sitting at a control booth, and suddenly the competitors let out more shocked gasps. Lonnie glanced back at the metal pole to see that it was now spinning.

"Who's the man?" Jay asked, patting his chest.

Lonnie rolled her eyes. "You're so conceited."

"Say it," Jay coaxed.

Lonnie crossed her arms. "I will not."

"Say it!" Jay nudged her with his elbow.

Lonnie sighed. "Fine. You are. You're the man. Happy?"

He flashed a wicked smile. "Yes, and I'll be even more happy after you *rock* this elimination round!"

Lonnie couldn't help sharing Jay's conviction. All those

years watching the Auradon Warrior Challenge had clearly paid off. He'd trained her well.

"Okay!" Ari announced, gathering the crowd's attention. "We will go in order of your competitor number. Starting with number one."

Lonnie remembered the number she had been assigned by the lady at the registration table—178—and sighed. This would take a while.

Lonnie and Jay took seats on a long bench that had been set up for the competitors as the first person took his mark on the course. For the next few hours, they watched competitor after competitor tackle the challenges. Most people were eliminated after the first obstacle, failing to grab on to one of the ropes and plunging into the water below. Some were knocked out by the Great Wall of Fire, the heat burning through their gloves and forcing them to drop. And only a few were able to conquer the Bridge of Despair. As more and more competitors were eliminated, Lonnie started to like her odds of making it to the final round the next day. And by the time her turn eventually arrived, she was feeling readier than ever.

"Okay," Jay said, turning to her to give her a quick pep talk. "You got this. I've done the math. You just have to finish the course in less than four minutes twenty-two seconds and you'll be guaranteed a spot in the finals tomorrow. Easy peasy."

" 'Easy peasy'?" Lonnie joked, jabbing him with a finger. "You've been spending too much time around AKs."

"I only surround myself with the very *best* AKs," he said with a grin.

Lonnie smiled. She was genuinely touched. Jay had spent so much of his free time helping her get here. She was feeling extremely grateful. "Thanks, Jay."

He playfully slapped her arm. "Enough sappiness! Now get out there and show them what you got!"

After the show broke for a commercial, a nearby producer motioned to Lonnie. "Competitor One Seventy-Eight. You're up. Please take your position at the start of the course."

Lonnie steeled herself and stood up, smoothing out her black warrior uniform. She knew she was supposed to get to the first obstacle and be ready to go by the time they came back from the commercial break. She took a deep breath and made her way toward the Monkey's Dare. She was just about to climb the steps to the platform when that same producer's voice called out to her across the arena, startling her. "Competitor One Seventy-Eight, where is your helmet?"

Lonnie touched her head and suddenly remembered she'd forgotten to put it on. She must have left it back on the bench.

She felt so foolish! How could she forget something as

important as that? The registration lady had already sternly warned her that she wouldn't be allowed on the course without it.

"Sorry!" Lonnie shouted and quickly ran back to her seat.

She expected Jay to be holding it up for her, but he was just looking at her with a blank expression.

"Where's my helmet?" she asked him.

He shook his head. "I don't know. I thought you had it."

"No!"

Together, they searched under the bench and all around it. Panic started to bloom in Lonnie's stomach. Where could her helmet have gone? She tried to think back to when she'd last seen it. She had definitely had it when she was entering the dome.

Hadn't she?

Or had she left it back in the Training Center?

"Competitor One Seventy-Eight!" the producer hissed at her. "Do you have your competition helmet? We are back to live in sixty seconds!"

"Uh . . . uh . . ." Lonnie stammered, feeling her heart pounding in her chest as she tried to figure out what to do. "I seem to have misplaced my helmet!"

Jay slammed his fist into his hand. "It was that Chen guy! He must have stolen it!"

"Don't be paranoid, Jay," Lonnie scolded. "I'm sure I just left it somewhere."

"I told you to watch out for that guy. I don't trust him. He's clearly trying to get you disqualified."

Lonnie shook her head. "That's ridiculous. They're not going to disqualify me just because—"

But just then, the producer interrupted her with a sad shake of his head. "I'm sorry, but we cannot allow you to participate in the Auradon Warrior Challenge without a helmet. If you don't have one, I'm afraid you'll be disqualified from the competition."

OBSTACLE

No! It can't be over! Not like this! I have to be able to compete. Otherwise, how will I convince the council to give me the sword of Shan-Yu?

Lonnie didn't know what she was supposed to do. She didn't have time to run back to the registration desk to get another helmet.

"I told you!" Jay growled through gritted teeth. "Just look at him gloating over there."

Lonnie glanced over at Chen, who was sitting farther down on the bench. He had a contented look on his face that made Lonnie's skin crawl. Could Jay be right? Was Chen really trying to sabotage her? Just because she'd beaten him on the Mountain of Doom?

No. She refused to believe that. This was Auradon.

People here were supposed to be kind and decent and good sports.

"We are live in forty-five seconds!" the producer called out. "We must get the next competitor onto the course."

"Wait!" someone shouted. "Li can use my helmet!"

Lonnie turned to see the female competitor who had congratulated her after beating Chen. She was holding up her helmet and waving it in the air.

See? Lonnie thought. *Kind and decent.*

"Thank you!" Lonnie cried, and she and Jay ran over to grab the helmet. "Thank you so much!"

The girl grinned. She looked to be only a little older than Lonnie. "I just want you to beat Chen at his own game."

Lonnie nodded. "I'll do my best."

"I'm Yi-Min," she said, "daughter of Yao."

"Daughter of Yao?" Lonnie said in surprise, recognizing the name. Her mother had told her stories about the fellow soldiers who had fought alongside her when she defeated Shan-Yu. "Your dad and my mom . . ." Lonnie began to say, but let her voice trail off. For a moment, she'd almost forgotten she was in disguise. "Um . . . they knew each other. Way back in the day."

Yi-Min smiled. "That's great! You better get out there before the producer has a heart attack."

Lonnie nodded and slid the borrowed helmet over her blond wig. "Thank you again!" she tried to say, but the words were muffled by the helmet, which Lonnie now noticed was gigantic on her. The top part was supposed to come down to her eyebrows, leaving her eyes, nose, and mouth uncovered. But it was way too big, and Lonnie's whole face was practically swallowed.

"Oh!" Yi-Min said. "I'm sorry. I've always had an exceptionally large head. I inherited that from my dad."

Lonnie pushed the helmet up on her forehead so she could see Yi-Min. "That's okay," she said, trying to sound grateful. After all, the girl had saved her from getting disqualified. "I'll make it work."

But as soon as she released the helmet, it thunked back down over her eyes.

This is going to make things more difficult, Lonnie thought. She turned to Jay, propping the helmet back up so she could see him. He suddenly didn't look so confident anymore.

"Be careful out there," Jay warned her. "Chen is up to something."

Lonnie sighed. "Relax. I'm telling you, it was just a misunderstanding. I'm sure my helmet is back in the Training Center."

Jay shook his head. "I don't think so. He has it out for you, and he's not going to stop until you're out of the way."

Lonnie tapped Jay on the forehead. "You VKs are so paranoid. This isn't the Isle of the Lost."

"Exactly," Jay said with a laugh. "It's the Auradon Warrior Challenge. It's worse."

"Competitor One Seventy-Eight! We are live in ten seconds!" the producer shouted desperately, his face turning an alarming shade of red.

"Coming!" Lonnie called, and raced toward the first obstacle, keeping her helmet propped up with one hand so she could see where she was going.

As she mounted the starting platform, she took a deep breath and looked out over the three obstacles she would have to undertake. The Monkey's Dare, the Great Wall of Fire, and the Bridge of Despair. She made one last attempt to adjust her helmet, finally managing to tilt it back and balance it precariously on her head so that it stayed in place and she could just barely see under the rim. It wasn't ideal, but it was better than nothing.

Okay, she told herself as she shuffled to the edge of the platform and grabbed on to the first rope. *You can do this.*

As she waited for the cameras to come back on and the producer to signal her to go, she glanced out into the crowd, wondering what was taking so long. She tried to catch Jay's eyes, but he was focused on something else. She followed his gaze to Chen, who was typing hastily into his phone, a furious expression on his face.

Finally Ari's voice came back over the arena speakers. "I'm sorry. We will need to extend our commercial break.

There's been a malfunction with the Bridge of Despair. Please wait momentarily while a technician fixes it."

A malfunction? Lonnie thought suspiciously. *How can that be? It's been working for the past one hundred seventy-seven competitors.*

She whipped her gaze toward the third obstacle, where the narrow metal pole had stopped spinning and a short man in a red AWC jumpsuit and cap was kneeling in front of the mechanism.

When Lonnie glanced back at Jay, he caught her eye and gave her a worried look.

Fear shot through Lonnie. Could that man be tampering with the course? She quickly brushed off the concern.

Jay's paranoia is rubbing off on you! she told herself. *Relax. He's just fixing it.*

But as the technician finished up his work, the cameras resumed the live feed, and the producer started the timer, signaling for Lonnie to begin, she couldn't shake the feeling that something was dreadfully wrong.

FIGHT TO THE FINISH

Okay, here goes everything!

One, two, three! Lonnie jumped from the platform, easily grabbing on to the first rope of the Monkey's Dare. She swung smoothly from rope to rope, using her body's momentum to keep her gliding forward. After all her practice with Jay, her grip was strong. The crowd cheered ecstatically as she reached for the final rope, the one that would swing her to the awaiting platform at the end of the obstacle.

But as soon as she grabbed on to it, her precariously positioned helmet shifted, falling back over her eyes. Lonnie could no longer see the top of the platform! All she could see was the inside of the gold helmet.

Her mind raced as she tried to figure out what to do. She could just jump toward the platform and hope her instincts guided her to the right place, but she risked missing the mark and falling into the water below, which would instantly disqualify her. On the other hand, if she didn't let go, she'd lose her momentum and be left dangling way too far away from the platform.

Lonnie's breath hitched in her chest. She just had to go for it. She'd seen other competitors hesitate before the end, and they were never able to build up enough power to reach the platform.

Lonnie let go of the rope. She felt herself flying through the air. But she could see nothing. Not the water below. Not the platform ahead. And not the shocked crowd who had all let out a simultaneous gasp when they'd realized what had happened.

Then, Lonnie felt a jolt and a bang as her feet hit something solid.

She'd made it! She'd landed safely on the platform. But without her vision, it was impossible for Lonnie to find her balance, and she quickly tumbled forward, her feet scuffing across the spongy surface. She tried to pull herself to a halt, but the force of her blind landing was too much and she kept stumbling forward. Then she heard someone cry out. "Lean back!"

It was Jay. He was guiding her.

Lonnie didn't hesitate. She did as she was told, thrusting her body backward until she fell onto her butt. But at least she'd stopped moving. She released a breath and pushed up her helmet. Her heart skipped when she saw how close to the edge of the platform she was. She'd nearly toppled right over the side into the water. The fall would have immediately eliminated her from the competition. She glanced at Jay, who was standing off to the side of the course, and gave him a grateful nod. He motioned for her to keep going. She was wasting precious time.

Lonnie jumped to her feet and peered at the giant timer on the wall. She was already a minute and forty-two seconds in. That little blindness episode had cost her some time. She'd have to make up for it in the next obstacle.

Lonnie ran toward the Great Wall of Fire, holding her helmet up with one hand as she went. When she reached the edge of the wall, she tentatively stuck her gloved hand out and placed it against one of the bricks. Even through the black leather of her glove, she could feel the heat. She wouldn't be able to keep her hands on the wall for more than a second without burning herself.

And then there was still the matter of this annoying helmet! Lonnie didn't know what she was going to do about that. There was no way she was going to get through this obstacle and the next one completely blind. If only there were something she could wedge between the helmet and her head. Something to fill up the extra space so the helmet didn't bounce around and fall over her eyes.

Something like . . .

Her gaze fell to her gloved hand, still lingering near the scorching hot wall.

Lonnie gulped. She had no other choice. She ripped her gloves off one at a time and quickly stuffed them up under the rim of her helmet. It worked. The hulking thing stayed in place, leaving Lonnie's eyes unobstructed.

Another gasp had permeated through the bleachers. No one could believe she was going to take on this wall without any gloves! She had to be crazy!

Just move fast and you won't feel it.

Lonnie thought back to the days Jay had made her walk barefoot across hot coals.

"The trick is to never stop moving, to never let your skin touch the coals for more than a split second," Jay had told her.

Lonnie knew the same technique applied here.

She'd already seen countless other competitors tackle this obstacle, and they had all moved in a hand-hand-foot-foot rhythm. But she couldn't do that. It would mean her hands would have to rest on the wall for too long, and she'd surely burn her skin.

She'd have to move her hands and feet at the exact same time, leaping horizontally across the two walls. It would definitely add a level of difficulty that she wasn't prepared for.

Lonnie closed her eyes, inhaled deeply, and imagined the sword of Shan-Yu. She pictured herself removing it from its protective glass case, holding it in her hands, showing it off to everyone at the induction ceremony.

Then she pictured that letter from the Imperial Council. The one that had told her she wasn't yet worthy of the sword. And that was all the motivation she needed.

Lonnie's eyes shot open and she leaped into the air, rotating her body sideways and wedging it between the two walls so her feet were pressed against one, her hands were pressed against another, and she was staring straight down at the deep ravine below.

The heat from the fiery wall immediately seared her bare hands and she let out a yelp of pain, but it was enough to get her moving. And fast.

Lonnie scurried between the two walls as rapidly as she could, moving in tiny leaps and never letting her hands linger against the scalding hot surface for too long. The heat on her palms and fingertips was so intense, it only pushed her to go faster. By the time she made it to the other side and glanced at the clock, she realized that she'd just completed the Great Wall of Fire faster than any of the competitors so far! Apparently, taking off her gloves had actually *helped*.

"*Yeah!*" Jay cheered from the sidelines. "That's my friend!"

She turned to flash him a beaming smile and then peered back at the clock.

03:30.

She had less than a minute to get to the end if she wanted a spot in that final round.

Lonnie turned and stared down the Bridge of Despair. She could see the final platform on the other side. Nothing stood between her and victory except an impossibly thin spinning pole.

You can do this, Lonnie told herself. *It's just like the log back at school.*

Lonnie took a deep breath to steady her nerves. She could hear Jay's voice in her head once again, telling her what to do.

The key to the spinning log is to never stop moving. Go fast or go home.

Right, Lonnie said to herself. *Never stop moving. Never stop—*

She took her first step onto the pole, preparing to run across it as quickly as she could, but the surface of the metal was surprisingly slick and her foot slid right out from under her.

Lonnie let out a scream as her body was flung to the side and she saw the water below come rushing toward her.

DON'T SWEAT THE TECHNIQUE

That was not part of the plan.
Also, this challenge is crazy hard.

Lonnie reached up quickly, and her fingers grasped the metal pole. She clutched it tightly, just managing to stop herself from falling.

Now, she was dangling. Which wasn't much better.

She could practically feel the water biting at her toes.

Lonnie knew she had to get her body back up onto that platform, but the pole was so slick, she was having trouble keeping her grip. *And* of course, it was still spinning. She kept having to readjust her hands with every rotation.

"Come on, you've got this!" she heard Jay call from the bleachers, and his voice gave her resolve. With a grunt, she used all her core strength to whip her legs upward, catching the pole between her ankles.

Yes!

But it was too early to celebrate. Lonnie still needed to get the rest of her body up.

The pole continued to turn. She tried to maneuver her hands and ankles to keep up with it. With another huge heave, Lonnie pulled herself up and scrambled backward to the safety of the starting platform.

She let out a sigh. That was close. Too close.

And strange, Lonnie thought. *Why did my foot slip in the first place?*

She glanced down at the spinning pole and noticed it looked . . . shiny. Much shiner than it should have been. She squatted down and ran her fingertip across the surface. It came back glistening with what smelled like . . .

Cooking oil?

In an instant, everything became clear.

Her missing helmet. Chen texting. The technician running out to "repair" the bridge.

Lonnie's mouth fell open in shock.

That little cheat!

Jay had been right. Chen *was* trying to sabotage her. He had sent someone out here to grease up the metal pole so she'd fall off! Did he have a friend who worked in the competition? Or was that guy in the red jumpsuit just posing as a real technician?

Either way, Lonnie was *angry.* And shocked. How could he do that? How could he try to cheat his way to another victory? That wasn't fair! And it certainly wasn't very Auradonian.

Just then, Lonnie caught sight of the clock and let out a squeak.

04:15!

She had exactly seven seconds to get across this slick pole in order to secure her spot in the finals! What was she going to do? How could she possibly get across this bridge? She knew that as soon as she took a single step, her foot would slide right off the pole again like a vegetable gliding across an oiled pan.

A vegetable gliding across an oiled pan . . .

The image hung in Lonnie's mind for a split second before the idea hit her. She had no time to think it through. No time to ponder whether it would work. It was her only option.

Never stop moving, she repeated in her mind. That had been Jay's advice, and that was exactly what she was going to do.

Lonnie backed up a few paces, checked to make sure her helmet was still secure, and ran toward the edge of the platform. Just before tumbling over the side, she jumped up and landed with her feet sideways on the pole. The momentum from the run, plus the grease from the cooking oil, sent her flying. She crouched down, keeping her center of gravity low and controlled, as though she were about to perform a killer hip-hop dance move. Then she glided straight across the bridge, like a surfer riding a wave back to shore.

It felt incredible. Like she was flying.

When she reached the other end, she jumped onto the platform, stopping the timer right at four minutes and twenty-one seconds.

The crowd went wild. She looked over to see Jay jumping up and down on the sidelines, high-fiving everyone in his vicinity.

"Well, that was certainly impressive!" Ari, the host, bellowed over the speakers. "Let's hear it for competitor one seventy-eight, who has officially qualified for the Auradon Warrior Challenge finals!"

Even though she was breathless and exhausted, Lonnie couldn't keep the smile off her face. She'd done it! She'd qualified!

Lonnie removed her borrowed helmet and waved to the cheering crowd. A member of the TV crew jumped up in front of her, pointing a camera right at her face. Lonnie self-consciously smoothed down her blond wig.

The show cut to commercial and the cameraman disappeared. Lonnie made her way back to the bench, where all her fellow competitors were on their feet, ready to high-five her. Well, all of them except Chen, of course. As she walked past him, she caught his gaze and held it. He was the only one in the entire arena not cheering for her. Instead, his face was twisted into a nasty scowl.

Lonnie did the only appropriate thing she could think of. She flashed Chen a wide grin and bowed.

VICTORY

I did it! I qualified for the Auradon Warrior Challenge! This. Is. Awesome.

"That rat! That cheat! That low-life, no-good, rotten hoodlum!"

It had been over an hour since the end of the elimination round, and Jay hadn't stopped ranting. Lonnie, Jordan, and Jay were all gathered in the plush living room of the royal suite that Lonnie had been assigned as one of the finalists.

"Wow, those are some choice words coming from a VK," Jordan joked.

But Jay ignored her and continued his rant against Chen. It was probably the first time since they'd left Auradon Prep that he hadn't had some flirty comeback for her. Even Jordan looked surprised.

"We need to turn him in," Jay said resolutely. He was

pacing the length of the living room while Jordan and Lonnie were lounging on the big, comfy white couch, eating pieces of fruit from the giant gift basket the producers of the show had sent.

"This royal treatment is pretty fantastic," Jordan said to Lonnie.

"Right?" Lonnie agreed. "I mean, this suite is amazing."

"Don't you mean it's *sweet*?" Jordan mocked, clearly trying to tease Jay about his joke earlier.

But Jay was barely listening. "We need to tell the producers," Jay said, mostly to himself. "But first we need proof that he was behind the sabotage. Otherwise, they'll never believe us."

"Did you see the fabulous earrings I found when I was out shopping today?" Jordan asked Lonnie, turning her head this way and that so Lonnie could see the large gold hoops dangling from her ears.

"Those are beautiful!" Lonnie gushed, and then turned to Jay, trying to distract him from his rant. "Jay, aren't Jordan's earrings beautiful?"

"Completely unacceptable," Jay went on, ignoring her. "He should be disqualified."

Jordan laughed. "We should order room service and watch movies." She plucked a red leather menu from the coffee table and flipped it open. "Oooh. They have chocolate-chip waffles!"

"I will find him and *make* him confess to the producers," Jay said, his fists balled at his sides.

"Oooh, chocolate-chip waffles are my favorite!" Lonnie enthused. "Do they have cream puffs?"

"They have a cream puff variety platter!" Jordan said, gawking at the menu.

"Done," Lonnie said, picking up the phone on the side table. "I'll order. Jay, do you want anything?"

But Jay was still lost in his vengeful world. "No one messes with me and my trainee and gets away with it. He cannot be allowed to continue with this competition!"

"Nothing? Okay!" Lonnie said, dialing the number for room service.

"Jay, will you relax?" Jordan urged.

Jay paused long enough to rub his hand against his forehead, where little beads of perspiration had formed. "I can't relax!" he called back. "This guy tried to sabotage Lonnie on the course!"

"Tried," Lonnie emphasized. "But didn't succeed." Then, into the phone, she said, "Oh, yes, hi. An order of chocolate-chip waffles and the cream puff variety platter, please. Thirty minutes? Great! Thanks so much!" She hung up and turned her attention back to Jay. "I still made it. I'm in the finals. So what does it matter?"

"It matters," Jay said through gritted teeth. "He can't get away with this. And what if he tries again?"

Lonnie shook her head. "He won't."

"Don't be so sure," Jay warned. "If he didn't succeed in knocking you out of the competition the first time, he's not going to just give up and let you win this whole thing."

Lonnie leaned back on the couch with a yawn. "I can't worry about that right now. I need to get my rest. And eat a platter full of yummy cream puffs."

"Well, I won't be able to sleep until I catch this guy," Jay said, stalking toward the door.

"Do what you gotta do," Jordan said with a roll of her eyes.

Jay stopped in the doorway and glanced back at Lonnie. "I will not let you down. Your knight in shining armor is on the job."

"She doesn't need a knight in shining armor!" Jordan called back, but it was too late. Jay had already disappeared out the door. Jordan let out a groan. "Why is he so annoying?"

Lonnie had started to get a pretty good idea of why Jay had been acting so ridiculous around Jordan during this whole trip, but she didn't want to get involved. Especially when she had a final round of competition to worry about tomorrow. So she just shrugged and said, "Who knows? He's a mysterious creature."

"He's a creature, all right." Jordan hopped up and started to explore the suite, walking from room to room and opening up all the closets and drawers. "OMG. They have silk robes in here!" she called from the bathroom. "I simply have to take a bath and put one of these on."

Lonnie giggled. "Knock yourself out."

"I'm going to put the genie lamp in the bedside table for safekeeping," Jordan said. "Don't let me forget it when we leave tomorrow."

"Okay!"

Then Lonnie heard the bathroom door close, followed by water running in the tub. Lonnie burrowed down farther into the plush white couch. It had to be the comfiest couch she'd ever sat on. She was so exhausted she could literally stay here all night and never move.

She reached for the remote, turned on the TV, and started flipping through the channels until she found one that was showing coverage from the day's event. On the screen, Snow White was interviewing Ari, the host of the Auradon Warrior Challenge.

"How did it go today in the elimination round?" Snow White asked. "Some of the footage I've seen was quite exciting!"

"Yes," Ari replied. "This is definitely shaping up to be our most thrilling challenge yet. We have some really strong competitors this year. A few familiar faces from previous years and a few surprises."

Just then, a clip of Lonnie gliding across the slick

metal pole played on-screen with the name "Li" written underneath. Lonnie was grateful not only for her blond wig, heavily made-up face, and fake name, but also for the oversized helmet, which seemed to disguise her even more. There was no way anyone back at school would recognize her as Lonnie. Or that anyone in the Imperial City would recognize her as the daughter of Mulan. She breathed a sigh of relief.

Her secret was safe.

She continued to watch the interview, listening to Ari's and Snow White's commentary on each of the ten finalists. But a few minutes later, her viewing was interrupted by a faint buzzing noise. Lonnie glanced down at the coffee table to see her phone lighting up with a text message. She reached for it and saw Mal's name on the screen. For a moment, Lonnie panicked, thinking someone back at school had recognized her on TV and Mal was texting to warn her of all the trouble she was already in.

But instead, the message said:

Had a wicked time filming the documentary last week. When do I get to see the edit you've been working on?

Lonnie stared at the screen in confusion. What was Mal talking about? What documentary? What edit? Lonnie wasn't working on a . . .

Then, suddenly, she glanced down at the fuchsia phone case in her hand and realized what had happened. This was Jordan's phone! They had the same case. Mal must be talking about the documentary Jordan had promised to produce for King Ben about the VKs.

But hadn't Jordan said she was going to wish to be free of that promise? That she didn't have time to do it? Isn't that why she had agreed to let Lonnie use the lamp in the first place—so she could get out of the commitment she'd made to Ben?

Lonnie thought back to the conversation she'd had with Jordan in the study room the night before.

"I just promised him I would produce a documentary about Mal, Evie, Jay, and Carlos so he could use it to bring more VKs to Auradon Prep."

"That sounds awesome!" Lonnie said. *"That'll definitely help him convince the rest of the royal council."*

Jordan shot her an uneasy look. "Yeah, well, I don't have the time. So I need to get out of it."

Lonnie was confused. She glanced down at the text message from Mal and read it again.

Jordan had already filmed the documentary? And she'd been editing it? Why, then, would she tell Lonnie that she didn't have time to work on it?

Lonnie remembered sensing that something was off when she'd talked to Jordan about it that night. She'd gotten the feeling that Jordan had been keeping some kind of secret from her.

And now Lonnie was more certain than ever that her feeling was right.

Lonnie looked to the closed bathroom door, her curiosity growing. She had to know what was going on. What was Jordan hiding? Lonnie knew she had to confront her and find out the truth. She decided to wait until Jordan was out of the bathtub and their stomachs were full of waffles and cream puffs. Then Lonnie would get to the bottom of this.

Fortunately, she wouldn't have to wait much longer, because just then there was a knock at the door.

IN THE CUT

I'm going to ask Jordan what's going on . . . as soon as I get the chance.

Lonnie was surprised to find not room service on the other side of the door, but an official Auradon Warrior Challenge staff member. He was dressed in the standard red jumpsuit with matching red cap. He handed Lonnie a gold envelope with the name "Li" printed on the front in black calligraphy, then bowed and turned to leave.

Lonnie closed the door and immediately opened the letter. She pulled out a crisp cream-colored card and read it.

Congratulations on becoming a finalist in the Auradon Warrior Challenge! To celebrate your impressive accomplishment, I'm personally hosting a celebratory gala for all finalists tonight at 8:00 p.m.

at the Silk Nightclub. Your attendance would be
greatly appreciated.
Yours truly,
Ari
Official AWC Host

Wow, Lonnie thought giddily. *A celebration gala at a*
nightclub? Hosted by Ari? That sounds so glamorous!

"Was that the food?" Jordan asked, stepping out of the
bathroom. She was now swathed in a gorgeous red and gold
silk robe, and her hair was twisted up in a towel.

"No, it was an invitation!" Lonnie said, handing Jordan
the card. "To a party!"

"Stellar," Jordan said, grabbing the card and reading
it. "I am *so* glad I went shopping today." She glanced up at
Lonnie and frowned at her face.

"What?" Lonnie said, self-consciously touching her
cheeks.

"I'll have to redo your makeup."

Lonnie walked over to the mirror in the living room and
suddenly realized what Jordan was scowling at. After all her
exertions in the arena today, her makeup looked pretty hor-
rific. And she had to maintain appearances if she was going
keep her true identity a secret.

The room service was delivered a few minutes later, and
the girls spent the next hour trying on outfits, touching up

makeup, and eating waffles and cream puffs. It was the best girls' night Lonnie could remember.

She hadn't forgotten her decision to ask Jordan about her wish, but she had yet to find the right moment to bring it up. Jordan seemed so excited about going to this party, and Lonnie didn't want to spoil her good mood. As hard as she tried, Lonnie still couldn't figure out why Jordan was so desperate to get out of producing the documentary. Had something happened during the filming to upset her? Was she mad at King Ben for some reason?

Lonnie was determined to find out . . . after this amazing gala, obviously.

When eight o'clock rolled around, Jordan and Lonnie were ready to rock. Lonnie's disguise had been completely renewed. Her wig had been brushed out and shined up with hair gloss, her vibrant makeup had been completely reapplied, and for clothes, she had decided to just stick to her black warrior uniform, which Jordan agreed was a nice touch.

"Should we wait for Jay to get back?" Lonnie asked as they opened the door to the suite.

"No way!" Jordan said, wrinkling her nose. "He'll just try to hit on all the female competitors."

Lonnie chuckled. "Yeah, but he *is* my trainer."

"Fine," Jordan said. "We'll text him from the party and tell him where we are."

"Perfect."

Jordan ordered a car from the Majestic Rides app and the two met their driver out front a few minutes later.

"The Silk Nightclub, please," Lonnie said, reciting the venue name from the invitation.

"Silk Nightclub?" the driver repeated with a twinge of confusion. "Didn't that club close last year?"

Lonnie shrugged. "Well, it's for a private party. So maybe they rented out the space."

The driver, seemingly satisfied with this answer, put the car in gear and pulled away from the Imperial Palace.

The Silk Nightclub was all the way on the other side of the city. Lonnie kept her face glued to the window as she took in the familiar sights of her hometown. Restaurants she used to eat at with her parents. The playground with the giant dragon-shaped jungle gym she used to climb on as a child. Even the shop where her mom had bought Lonnie her very first suit of armor. It was all still there.

When the car dropped them in front of the large warehouse-style concrete building on the outskirts of the city, Lonnie and Jordan could hear the music thumping from the inside. It had been a long time since Lonnie had let loose with her hip-hop moves, and she was eager to get on that dance floor.

"This is gonna be great!" she said to Jordan as they headed for the door. They pulled open the heavy metal door

and stepped into the large, open space. But the girls both stopped in their tracks when they saw that the entire building was empty. And almost pitch-dark. The only light was coming from the open door that they'd just walked through.

"Are we the first to arrive?" Lonnie asked, glancing around. She'd expected to see spinning disco balls, long tables full of fancy foods, and cocktail servers walking around with gold trays.

"Maybe," Jordan said. "That's weird. The invitation said eight o'clock, didn't it?"

Lonnie reached into her pocket to find the invitation, but then realized she must have left it back in the room. She couldn't even remember where she'd last seen it. "I think so. But where is everyone?"

They took a few more steps inside, and that's when Lonnie noticed the small speaker in the corner blasting the music they'd heard from the outside.

That's strange, she thought. She had expected there to be a DJ, with equipment at *least* as high-tech as her own DJ equipment.

So far, this party was *not* turning out to be as glamorous as she thought. No food. No DJ. And no people.

"Maybe we should leave," Jordan suggested.

Lonnie had to agree with Jordan. She was starting to think maybe the driver had taken them to the wrong place. Plus, this building was kind of giving her the creeps.

"Yeah," Lonnie said. "Let's go. We'll call another Majestic Ride."

The two girls turned around just in time to see the door to the outside slam shut, thrusting them into darkness.

Uh-oh, Lonnie thought.

She heard Jordan jiggling the door handle. "It's locked."

"It can't be," Lonnie said, stumbling up through the blackness and pushing Jordan aside. She tried the handle for herself, twisting it with all her might. She even tried kicking the door a few times and pushing it with all her strength, but nothing worked. They were definitely locked in here.

Then, through the darkness, they heard a cackle of laughter, followed by a chillingly familiar voice. "That was almost too easy."

Lonnie's heart began to race. It was Chen. She knew it.

She ran her fingers across the wall near the door until she came across an air vent no bigger than a textbook. She flipped it open, letting in a sliver of light, and peered through the slats.

Sure enough, just as she expected, outside the empty club stood Chen. He leaned down toward the vent, flashing his obnoxious smirk at Lonnie.

"Chen," Lonnie said sternly. "Open this door right now. You don't want to do this."

"Oh, but I do," Chen said snidely. "I can't let you take my title from me. The Auradon Warrior Challenge is *my* competition. It has been for the past four years, and it will be mine again. I'm about to make history, and you're not going to stand in my way."

"You'll get caught," Lonnie warned him.

Through the narrow slats, Lonnie could see Chen twisting his mouth to the side as though contemplating her statement. "I don't think so. Besides, it won't matter. The final competition starts in twelve hours, and no one is coming way out here to this abandoned club to look for you. I'm afraid to say you won't be competing tomorrow."

"Listen to me, you little rat!" Jordan said, pushing her way to the air vent. "You let us out of here right now, or I'll . . . I'll . . ."

Chen laughed. "You'll what? What are either of you going to do about it?"

Both Lonnie and Jordan remained silent.

"That's exactly what I thought," Chen said. "Don't worry. I'll make sure someone comes to find you tomorrow *after* the competition is over."

Lonnie heard footsteps fading into the distance. "Nighty night!" Chen called out, followed by a dark, chilling silence.

LOW BLOW

Well, now I know the truth. Jay was
totally right. Chen fights dirty.

"Hello! Somebody! Anybody! We're in here!" Lonnie and
Jordan screamed at the top of their lungs through the air
vent, but it was no use. No one had any idea they were down
here. Jay didn't even know they'd left. There was no way
he'd be able to find them. They were definitely trapped.

They both seemed to realize this at the same time and
stopped shouting.

"Wait, what about your phone?" Jordan asked. "You
can call Jay. Or text him!"

Lonnie quickly pulled her phone out of her pocket only
to find that there were no service bars on her screen.

"No reception. Must be the concrete walls."

"Wi-Fi?" Jordan suggested.

Lonnie did a search. "No Wi-Fi. It's like the Isle of the Lost in here."

She flipped on the phone's flashlight and quickly scanned the room. It was mostly empty apart from a few life-size marble statues and a couple of giant crystal chandeliers hanging from the ceiling. "All this stuff must be left over from the nightclub that used to be here."

"Fabulous," Jordan said sarcastically. "So we're in a junkyard. This really *is* the Isle of the Lost."

Lonnie glanced around and felt a shiver travel through her. She'd always prided herself on being brave, but some of these marble statues were pretty eerie. The ones shaped like humans seemed to be watching Lonnie and Jordan, while the others—shaped like dragons and tigers—looked ready to pounce. They cast strange, creepy shadows in the light of her phone. Lonnie was reminded of the time she had gone to the Isle of the Lost with Jay and Carlos to fight the pirates that were holding Ben captive.

Lonnie shivered and turned off the screen. She couldn't believe she'd let this happen. She couldn't believe she had fallen for Chen's trap! How could she have been so foolish? Especially after he had clearly tried to sabotage her in the elimination round. Jay had been right when he'd said Chen would try again. Lonnie had just been too blind—or too naive—to believe it.

But it didn't really matter how she'd fallen for this trick. What mattered now was that they figure out a way to get out.

"Okay, think," Lonnie said to herself. "Think. Think. Think. Being a warrior is all about strategy. Mental maneuvering."

"Oh, yeah," Jordan sneered. "Some mental maneuvering you did. You're the one who got us in this mess."

Lonnie ignored her and kept thinking. Then, a moment later, she was struck with an idea. "The lamp!" she yelled suddenly. "I still have a second wish!" She squeezed her eyes shut tight and said, "Jordan, I wish for you to get us out of here."

Lonnie held her breath and waited.

And waited.

And waited.

Nothing happened. There was no tingling feeling. No pink smoke. Nothing. When she opened her eyes, the thin shaft of light from the air vent was just enough for her to make out Jordan staring at her with her arms crossed and a sour expression on her face.

"What happened?" Lonnie asked.

"The lamp's not here, genius!" Jordan said, throwing her arms up. "It's back in the suite. Your wish only works if you're holding the lamp."

Lonnie's shoulders slouched. "Oh."

"Any other brilliant ideas?"

Lonnie felt her temper flare. She remembered Jay's pep talk about staying calm. Not letting your emotions get the better of you. Warriors don't act from anger. "Jordan," she said calmly. "Now is not the time to turn against each other. We need to work together. We need to figure out how to get out of here."

Jordan sighed. "You're right. I'm sorry." She collapsed against the locked door and slid to the ground. "I never should have put the lamp in that drawer. I should have kept it on me. Dad always told me, never let your lamp out of your sight. Otherwise it could fall into the wrong hands. That's what happened with Jafar, and it nearly ruined everything."

Lonnie chuckled at the irony of that as she sat down next to Jordan. "And yet, now I'd give anything for it to fall into Jafar's *son's* hands. Jay would certainly use it to help us get out."

"Well, Jay is different from his father." Jordan went quiet for a moment. "In fact, all the VKs at Auradon are different from their parents."

"Then why have you been so mean to him lately?" Lonnie asked.

Jordan shook her head and refused to make eye contact with Lonnie. "It's a long story."

"Something tells me we're going to be here awhile," Lonnie pointed out.

Jordan barked out a laugh. "I guess you're right." Then she sighed. "We got into this stupid fight, and he said something to me that was really mean and hurtful, and I got angry. Now he's been acting all weird around me, trying to impress me and stuff, because he knows I'm still mad at him. It's super annoying."

"What did he say?" Lonnie asked, shocked. She hadn't heard about this at all.

Jordan sighed. "It was when I was filming him for the documentary, and he said . . ." But her voice trailed off, and even through the darkness, Lonnie saw Jordan's eyes go wide. She knew Jordan had said something she hadn't meant to say.

Lonnie thought back to the text message she'd seen from Mal earlier that night, and she knew now was the time to get some answers.

"Jordan," Lonnie said gently. "I know you already filmed the documentary."

Jordan was silent for a moment. "How do you know that?"

"I mistook your phone for mine and saw a text message from Mal. It said something about how much fun she'd had filming and how she couldn't wait to see the edit you've been working on."

Jordan buried her face in her hands. "Okay, okay," she finally admitted. "I did it. I filmed it. I've even edited most of it together, but . . ." Her voice cracked, and for a moment Lonnie worried that Jordan wasn't going to finish her sentence. "But I don't *want* to finish it. And I definitely don't want Ben to use it to try to get more VKs into Auradon."

Lonnie was speechless. This wasn't at all what she'd expected Jordan to say.

"So that's why I need you to use your final wish to get me out of it."

"B-b-but," Lonnie stammered, still nearly too shocked to speak. "Why don't you want Ben to use it? Don't you want more VKs in Auradon? I thought you *liked* the VKs."

"I do!" Jordan insisted. "That's the problem!"

"I don't understand." Lonnie turned and stared at her friend. She could have sworn she saw tears streaming down Jordan's cheeks, but she couldn't be sure in this low light. What she *was* sure about, however, was that she'd never seen Jordan cry before. "Why wouldn't you want Ben to use your documentary?"

"Because . . ." Jordan wiped her eyes with the back of her hand. "Because I'm afraid."

"Afraid?" Lonnie repeated, certain she'd misunderstood. She couldn't imagine sassy, bold Jordan being afraid of anything.

Jordan laughed. "I know it's hard for someone like you to understand. *Afraid* is probably not even in your vocabulary."

Lonnie lowered her gaze to the floor. "I'm not so sure about that," she whispered.

But evidently Jordan hadn't heard her, because she kept talking. "This documentary is *so* important. It has to be incredible. The lives of other VKs are going to depend on it. What if it's bad? What if it fails, and then no one else can get off the Isle of the Lost? It'll be all my fault."

Lonnie forced a smile. "Jordan. I'm sure it's not bad. I've seen every episode of your web show, and they're *all* incredible. I'm sure the documentary is going to be incredible, too."

Jordan bit her lip. "I just can't take the chance that you're wrong. I can't risk failing."

"But if you give up now, don't you automatically fail?" Lonnie reasoned. "Isn't trying and failing better than not trying at all?"

Jordan shook her head adamantly. "No. Not when my reputation is on the line. Not to mention all those VKs I'd be letting down, too. I just can't handle that kind of pressure. I'd rather just use my wish to get out of my promise to Ben and forget this whole documentary even existed in the first place."

After that, they both fell silent for a long time. Lonnie had no idea how to respond to that. Especially when she realized she could relate to everything Jordan was saying. Lonnie suddenly remembered something Jay had said to her when he first mentioned the Auradon Warrior Challenge.

"What are you afraid of?" he'd asked. And Lonnie had quickly replied, "Nothing!"

But Jay had been so certain. "You're afraid of something," he'd told her.

At the time, Lonnie hadn't wanted to believe Jay, but now, sitting in this dark, creepy room, listening to Jordan echo her very fears, she realized Jay was right. She was afraid of something.

The same thing Jordan was afraid of.

Failure.

Lonnie fidgeted with the hem of her black jacket. "You're wrong, you know?" she whispered, half hoping that Jordan wouldn't hear her again.

But evidently she did.

Jordan scoffed. "Yeah, yeah, my web shows are great, blah blah blah."

"No," Lonnie said. "I meant you're wrong about me not being afraid."

Jordan turned to face Lonnie, and Lonnie could feel her inquisitive gaze. "What are you talking about?"

"I'm afraid of failing, too."

Jordan laughed as though she thought Lonnie were

making a joke. "You? The R.O.A.R. captain? Miss I-Fight-Pirates-on-the-Isle-of-the-Lost-in-My-Free-Time? *You're* afraid of failure?"

"Why do you think I wanted you to do my makeup and disguise me as someone else?"

Jordan frowned. "To avoid getting caught. Just like you said."

"That's part of it," Lonnie admitted. "But also, I really didn't want anyone to recognize me as Mulan and Shang's daughter. Especially if I lost." Lonnie let out a loud breath. "All my life I've grown up with these famous warriors as parents. That's a lot to live up to. And all my life, I've carried around this fear that I never will. It's like having an older sister or brother who's good at *everything*. Except it's not my sister. It's my mom *and* my dad. Do you know how embarrassing it would be if I turned out to be not as brave as the famous Mulan? Not as strong as her? Not as"—Lonnie swallowed the lump that was forming in her throat—"*worthy* as her?" She paused, letting that word hang heavily in the air. "Which is why I decided to enter the competition as someone else. Just in case I didn't win. That way I'd have less to lose."

Lonnie pulled her knees up to her chin and wrapped her arms around her legs. "I guess it doesn't matter now. It doesn't look like I'm going to get to compete tomorrow anyway. We're clearly not getting out of this room. No one will ever think to look for us way out here."

Jordan reached out to tuck a strand of Lonnie's blond wig behind her ear. "For what it's worth, I don't think you have any reason to be afraid."

Lonnie smiled. "For what it's worth, I don't think *you* do, either."

Lonnie watched her friend's expression carefully. She could tell that even though her words were touching Jordan, they weren't doing anything to convince her. And she really couldn't blame Jordan for that. Lonnie understood fear of failure.

She rested her head on Jordan's shoulder. "I promise, no matter what happens tomorrow, I'll still get you out of that commitment. I'll still use my third wish to set you free."

"Thank you," Jordan said, but the word was stifled by a yawn.

Lonnie yawned, too. She was so tired after all the events of the day. She vowed to stay awake, though. After all, she was a warrior. And warriors didn't fall asleep on the job. So while Jordan curled up on the floor and started to nod off, Lonnie stood up and started pacing the length of the club, searching for hidden exits or covered windows. She even walked around the entire space with her phone in search of a signal, but her screen still showed no connection.

Finally, she gave up and sat down next to Jordan. She wouldn't sleep. She would stay up and keep watch. Just in case anyone showed up. But as soon as she rested her head against the wall, she felt her eyelids grow heavy. She fought as hard as she could against the fatigue that threatened to pull her under, but soon, Lonnie was asleep.

LOOK SHARP

I may have fallen asleep, but that doesn't mean I'm giving up.

"Lonnie! Jordan! Are you in there?"

Lonnie struggled to open her eyes. Her whole body felt sore and heavy from the elimination round the day before. She was groggy and exhausted, but she could have sworn she heard Jay's voice. Although it was probably just her imagination. Or a dream.

Oh, gosh, she'd had the most terrible dream! She'd dreamed that Chen had led them into a trap, and they had gotten locked in a creepy old nightclub—

Lonnie glanced around her and shuddered.

It wasn't a dream. It was real!

She clicked on her phone to look at the time and sat bolt upright. It was eight in the morning! The final competition was starting in thirty minutes! They'd slept the whole night and were still locked in this horrible place.

She'd never get her sword now. Not if they were still stuck in here. She couldn't imagine how they'd ever be able to get out.

Why, oh, why hadn't they just stayed at Auradon Prep for the Study Lock-In? She'd much rather be locked in the dorms right now studying for Auradon History than locked in this creepy old building!

"Lonnie! Jordan! Can you hear me?"

Lonnie froze and turned her ear toward the door.

Was that . . . ?

"Hello! Anyone here?"

It wasn't a dream! He's really here!

Lonnie lunged for the air vent next to the door. "Jay! Jay! We're in here! Over here!"

"What's happening?" Jordan called out sleepily. "Why are you yelling?"

"It's Jay!" Lonnie called. "He's here!"

Jordan was up and next to Lonnie in a flash. "Jay!" she called through the slats.

"Jordan?" Jay called back. They could hear his voice, but they still couldn't see him from their limited view.

"In here! The air vent!"

Finally they saw Jay racing around the side of the

building. He skidded to a halt upon seeing their faces through the narrow gaps in the wall.

"How did you find us?" Lonnie asked.

Jay bent down to show them the invitation to the fake gala in his hands. "I found this in the bathroom of the suite. I'd been searching for you guys all night, and then I noticed my hair was looking a little ratty, so I went to borrow Jordan's brush and—"

"Ew," Jordan interrupted. "You borrowed my brush?"

"Hey," Jay said, giving his hair a toss. "You gotta take care of the hair."

Jordan rolled her eyes.

"Anyway," Jay went on. "When I saw the invitation, I figured you guys came here. But what are you doing in an air vent?"

"We're not *in* an air vent, you idiot," Jordan said. "We're talking *through* an air vent. We're stuck in this creepy old shut-down nightclub."

"Chen?" Jay said through gritted teeth.

Lonnie sighed. "He's the one who lured us here with the invitation."

"I can't believe that guy!" Jay yelled. "I've been looking for *him* all night, too, but I can't find him anywhere! I swear, I'm gonna get that hoodlum."

"First, how about you get *us* out of *here*?" Jordan suggested.

"The final competition starts in less than half an hour!" Lonnie cried.

"Crud," Jay swore. "Okay. I'll see if I can break the door down."

"Already tried that," Lonnie said.

"Yes, but you're a . . ."

"A girl?" Lonnie replied snidely. "Yeah, a girl who qualified for the Auradon Warrior Challenge, so what's the next plan?"

Jay huffed. "I'll go find someone with keys."

Lonnie shook her head. "There's no time for that." She felt tears well up in her eyes. She quickly blinked them away. She couldn't believe she had come this far and worked so hard just to have to forfeit.

"Wait," Jay said suddenly, as though he'd been struck with an idea. "Why don't you use your second wish and wish your way out?"

"She can't," Jordan said impatiently. "We don't have the lamp."

Jay grinned and took off his backpack, rifling inside for something. A second later, he pulled out a shiny golden object. "Oh, you mean *this* lamp?"

Jordan gasped. "You stole my lamp?"

Jay shrugged. "What can I say? Old habits die hard."

"You little thief!" Jordan yelled.

"Relax," Jay said. "I'm kidding. When I came back to

the room to find you guys were gone, I took it just in case. A VK is always prepared."

"Yeah," Jordan said, "whatever. Can you just give it to Lonnie?"

"Well, well," Jay said, cocking an eyebrow. "Look who needs a knight in shining armor now."

"I most certainly do *not*," Jordan said, crossing her arms. "And if you think this whole rescue thing is going to gain you any points with me, you're wrong."

"Fine," Jay said, taking a step back and admiring the lamp. "You can just stay in there."

"Fine," Jordan snapped.

"Um, guys," Lonnie interrupted. "Can we continue this argument later? I kind of need to get up to that arena."

Jay seemed to snap to attention. "Right. Sorry, Lonnie." He looked toward the vent and hesitated. "Um, how am I going to give this to you? This will *not* fit between these slats."

Lonnie suddenly got an idea and turned on her phone. She shined the flashlight toward the air vent. "Look!" she said, pointing at four tiny screws that were holding the plate in place. "The screws are on this side. Maybe I can unscrew them with something and you can pass us the lamp!"

"Great idea," Jordan muttered sarcastically. "But what are you going to unscrew them with? It's not like I bring screwdrivers to every gala I go to."

The group fell silent for a moment. Lonnie could practically hear the clock ticking from the arena.

"How about your earrings?" Jay suggested a moment later.

"I'm not wearing earrings," Lonnie replied.

"No, Jordan's earrings. The new hoopy ones she bought yesterday. They looked like they might be thin enough to wedge into the grooves of the screw."

Jordan touched the gold hoops dangling from her ears. "I didn't even think you were paying attention to our conversation."

Jay shrugged. "What can I say? They looked expensive."

Jordan groaned. "Is stealing really *all* you can think about?"

"Hey, you can take the guy out of the isle, but you can't take the isle out of the guy."

"Charming," Jordan mumbled.

"Let's just try it!" Lonnie screeched. "We're running out of time."

Jordan sighed and pulled the hoops out of her ears. She gave one to Lonnie, and they both went to work on the air vent.

"It fits!" Lonnie exclaimed, wedging the hoop into the screw and twisting. "They're coming out!"

Less than thirty seconds later, Lonnie and Jordan had

managed to get the plate off the air vent, leaving a rectangular hole in the wall just big enough for Jay to shove the lamp through.

Lonnie caught it and quickly rubbed the side.

"Now, Lonnie," Jordan said in a warning tone, "remember what I said before. Wishes are very complex things. The key is specificity. You should think very carefully before you—"

"Get us out of here!" Lonnie cried hastily.

Jordan pursed her lips. "Or you can just go with that."

Lonnie closed her eyes and felt the shimmery pink smoke billow around her. *Hurry*, she willed it with her mind. She could feel its silky heat against her skin and taste its smoky aroma in her mouth. When she opened her eyes again, she and Jordan were on the other side of the door, standing next to a scowling Jay.

"Really?" Jay asked in disbelief. "*That's* what you wished for?"

"What?" Lonnie asked, confused.

"You *could* have wished to take us to the arena. It's all the way across town."

Lonnie's gaze dropped to the lamp in her hands. "Oh. Whoops."

"I told you. Be specific!" Jordan said, taking the lamp back from Lonnie and storing it in her purse for safekeeping.

"I'm sorry!" Lonnie said defensively. "I was kind of in a hurry."

"Don't worry," Jordan said. "I'll order another Majestic Ride." She turned on her phone. "Finally! Signal!" Then she navigated to the Majestic Rides app, but a moment later scowled at the screen. "Dang it. There are no cars in the area. They must all be at the arena. It says it'll take thirty-five minutes to get one."

"We'll have to go by foot," Jay said.

Lonnie nodded and tried to psych herself up. She was a warrior, after all. She would not let a little transportation problem get her down.

"It's okay," she said confidently. "I grew up in this city. I know a few shortcuts. Follow me."

HIT BACK

*Even with all the shortcuts I know,
the arena is pretty far away,
and we're running out of time.*

As they ran through the Imperial City, over footbridges and through outdoor marketplaces, Lonnie continued to check the time on her phone, quickly coming to the conclusion that they weren't going to make it.

"We need to find a ride," Lonnie said, stopping to catch her breath. Jay and Jordan stopped behind her, each one seeming grateful for the break.

Lonnie glanced around. Parked across the street was a small red van with a white sign on the side that read "Dim Sum Delights." It was sitting just outside a restaurant with the same name. She watched as a young man carrying four large paper bags walked out of the restaurant. Each bag had a white piece of paper stapled to the front. The man placed all four bags in the back of the delivery van.

"Hey," Lonnie said, an idea forming in her mind. "Check out that van, you guys."

"Good eye!" Jay said, walking toward the vehicle. "We'll hotwire it."

Lonnie groaned and grabbed Jay by the arm. "No. I have a better idea."

She waited until the deliveryman finished loading the bags into the back of the van and closed the door. "C'mon, follow me!" she told Jordan and Jay, and dashed across the street. As the driver got into the van, Lonnie quietly eased open the back door and hopped in. Jay and Jordan followed, and Lonnie closed the door behind them carefully, trying to keep it from slamming.

The back of the van had no windows, so it was pretty dark inside. Lonnie used the flashlight on her phone to study the white pieces of paper stapled to the brown paper bags.

"What exactly are we doing?" Jordan asked.

"We used to order from this place all the time when I was a kid," Lonnie said. "They have the best dumplings."

Jay and Jordan exchanged glances. "Um," Jordan said warily, "I'm pretty hungry, too, Lonnie. But now's not exactly the time to be thinking about food."

Lonnie rolled her eyes. "I'm not stealing the food. I'm reading the addresses on the delivery receipts." She pointed to one of the bags. "This one is definitely closest to the arena. It's only a block away. There's a major intersection right before the address. Once he stops there, we can hop out and run the rest of the way."

Jay nodded approvingly. "Nice thinking. But what if he stops at one of the other addresses first?" He gestured toward the other three bags. "We don't exactly have time for pit stops. Plus, don't you think he'll find it a little strange opening up his van to discover three stowaways?"

Lonnie twisted her mouth to the side. Jay had a good point. She quickly reexamined the addresses on the three other receipts, trying to picture the map of the city in her mind. She'd lived here most of her life, but it had been a while since she'd had to make her way around the Imperial City.

The van began to rumble as the driver started the engine and pulled away from the curb. Lonnie closed her eyes and tried to focus on the movement of the vehicle. It went straight, then turned left, then right; then she felt a familiar bumpy sensation beneath them. *Bum-di-di-bump-bump.* And Lonnie felt her hopes soar.

"I know where he's going!" she shouted.

Jay looked impressed. "You do?"

"He just crossed the railroad tracks. And now he's turning left. I know exactly which route he's taking. There's no way he'll stop at the other addresses first. We just have to make sure we jump out—"

Just then the van screeched to a halt, and Lonnie, Jay, and Jordan lurched across the back. Lonnie reached out her hand to stop herself from flying into the wall. "Now!" she called. "This is the intersection!" She crawled toward the back of the van and twisted the handle, and all three of them jumped out and started racing down the block toward the front entrance of the arena.

As soon as they burst through the doors, Lonnie could hear the voice of Ari, the host, over the loudspeaker, welcoming everyone again to the annual Auradon Warrior Challenge. The opening ceremonies had already begun. She ran faster.

Just before they reached the competitors' entrance, Jordan pulled Lonnie to a stop. "Wait. Just a second."

Lonnie bounced on her heels. She was already so late! They were about to introduce the finalists! "What is it?" she asked impatiently.

Jordan pulled the lamp out of her purse and thrust it into Lonnie's hands. "Take this with you. Just in case you need to use your third wish."

Lonnie's eyebrows furrowed. "But the third wish is for you."

"I know," Jordan said, "but you've come so far. I'd hate for you to lose your sword."

Lonnie shook her head and pushed the lamp back to Jordan. "No. As soon as I win this thing, I'm using that third wish for you. Besides, I don't want to win the sword that way. I don't want to cheat my way to a victory. That would make me no better than Chen."

"Fine," Jordan said, but she still thrust the lamp back to Lonnie. "Then take it for luck. So you'll have a piece of me with you when you're out there."

Lonnie smiled tenderly at her friend and slipped the lamp inside her black jacket. It was bulky, but Lonnie was glad to have it with her. "Okay," she said. "For luck."

"And now it's time to meet our finalists!" Ari was saying.

Jordan gave Lonnie a gentle push. "Go. Win this thing!"

Lonnie gave her a thumbs up and took off toward the competitors' entrance. As soon as she entered the center of the arena, she saw the spectacle that lay in front of her. It was even wilder than the previous day's event! The bleachers were crammed full of people. Every single seat was taken. There were also hundreds of cameras and crew members set up around the various parts of the arena. In the center, the obstacle course had been replaced by another mysterious structure that was, once again, hidden from view by a massive white sheet. Lonnie remembered what Jay had told her about the final round. You could never prepare for it. You could never predict it. It was always a surprise.

She felt her stomach clench with anxiety. What was under that sheet?

Lonnie touched her wig to make sure her disguise was still in place. Thank goodness Jordan had reapplied her makeup the night before. Even though she'd slept in it, it was mostly intact.

"And our tenth and final competitor is Li!" Ari announced, eliciting wild cheers from the crowd.

Up ahead, where Ari and the rest of the competitors were standing, Lonnie saw Chen smugly walk up to Ari and whisper something into his ear.

Lonnie bowed her head and ran faster around the arena.

"Oh," Ari said with disappointment. "Unfortunately, it looks like Li was unable to make it to the final round this morning, and therefore—"

"I'm here! I'm here!" Lonnie shouted, rounding the bend. "I'm so sorry I'm late."

"I am misinformed!" Ari exclaimed. "It appears our bright new star, Li, has arrived just in time."

As Lonnie walked down the row of competitors to take her spot at the end, she could feel Chen's glare on her. "How did you get out?" he hissed under his breath as she passed by.

Lonnie grinned back at him. "The same way you got me in. With a little help from friends."

Chen looked so angry he seemed to be having trouble breathing.

"Shall we see what our competitors will be battling today?" Ari announced, sending the crowd into a tizzy. Lonnie's heart began to gallop in her chest.

"Unveil the final warrior challenge!"

BLOW FOR BLOW

This is it. It's time to prove I can beat that cheater Chen, and that I'm the most skilled warrior here.

The white sheet floated gracefully up into the air, revealing a sight unlike anything Lonnie had ever seen in her life. It was a giant structure made out of tall steel beams and a series of planks that hung from ropes, like wooden swings. They were only a few feet wide and not very long. They were located at various heights across the structure, some almost touching the ground, others high in the air. Lonnie's eyes traveled all the way to the top, to the highest platform that swung gently from its ropes, her stomach clenching at the sight of it.

What was she supposed to do with that?

Ari's voice came back over the speaker system just then. "Welcome," he said in an ominous voice, "to the Mountain of the Blazing Suns!"

The crowd let out a simultaneous "ooh!" while the competitors just stared speechlessly at the structure, waiting for Ari to explain what they would have to do.

"This final-round challenge will test not only the competitors' balance and reflexes, but also their skills with a sword."

Sword? Lonnie thought, hope rising in her chest. *Did he say* sword?

Just then, one of the show's producers appeared, pushing a giant wheelbarrow that was filled with ten gleaming metal swords. He handed one to each of the competitors. When Lonnie felt the weight of the weapon in her hand, she was immediately reminded of why she was here—the sword of Shan-Yu, waiting for her in the Hall of Wisdom—and she felt her resolve strengthen.

"Each competitor will have sixty seconds on the mountain," Ari went on, "during which they must destroy as many blazing suns as possible."

Titters of curiosity traveled through the rows of spectators. All of them were anxious to know what that meant. Lonnie included.

"This," Ari said dramatically, "is a blazing sun!"

And just then, something bright and glowing shot into the air and flew toward the giant structure in the center of the arena. It looked like a ball made of red-hot flames. It sailed in a perfect arc as though fired from a cannon. The crowd let out another gasp of excitement as the ball—or rather, blazing sun—landed on one of the wooden platforms, disintegrating almost instantly in a spark of light.

Lonnie was reminded of the dragon cannon balls that players had to duck on the tourney field. Jay had made her practice dodging them a few times. But this was different. She wasn't supposed to avoid them; she was evidently supposed to destroy them with her sword, *while* balancing on those swinging platforms.

This was going to be hard. Very hard.

"The competitor who destroys the most suns," Ari continued, "will win the title of Auradon Warrior Challenge Champion, as well as the official championship medal and the grand cash prize!"

Cash prize?

Lonnie had forgotten there even *was* a cash prize. Not that it mattered. She didn't really need the money, nor did she care about the medal. All she wanted was to be able to march up to that Imperial Council and demand her birthright.

"First up!" Ari announced. "Our reigning champion, Chen!"

Chen leaped into action, pumping his fists and waving at the crowd. They returned the salutation with a roar of applause. Apparently, he was not only the reigning champion, but also the crowd favorite.

Lonnie felt her temper flare while she watched him approach the structure. She was still angry at him for locking them inside that building, and also angry at herself for falling for his trap. But she remembered Jay's advice about not letting her emotions fuel her. She took deep breaths in an attempt to keep her temper in check.

Chen strode confidently toward the "mountain" and climbed onto the lowest plank. It swung under his weight and he had to hold on to the ropes with one hand to keep from falling off, while the other raised his sword in the air, ready for action.

A loud bell rang out across the dome and the clock on the wall started counting down from sixty seconds. The first blazing sun came swiftly. Chen jumped to the next-highest plank and easily sliced through the sun with his sword. The remnants of the once-glowing ball of light fell to the ground in an impressive shower of sparks and embers, like the tail end of a firecracker after it's exploded.

The next ball was fired shortly after, and Chen had to leap up two of the planks to reach it, but he easily destroyed that one as well.

Lonnie turned her attention toward the clock, which showed forty-five seconds remaining. Next to the clock was

a counter displaying the number of blazing suns Chen had already conquered—two. Now three. Now four.

Lonnie's gaze swiveled constantly between Chen and the counter on the wall, which seemed to rise faster with each passing second. Chen leaped agilely around the structure, swinging his sword with certainty, precision, and grace.

By the time the clock ran out and a buzzer sounded, Chen had managed to rack up twenty-two suns.

Lonnie glanced down the row at her fellow competitors. They all looked defeated before they'd even had a chance to compete.

Twenty-two was definitely the number to beat.

Except no one seemed to be able to come close. One by one, the competitors climbed onto the structure with their swords poised and ready, and one by one they failed to top Chen's feat.

The closest anyone else came was seventeen!

Lonnie was beginning to lose hope. She glanced down at the sword in her hand, knowing she'd need to destroy twenty-three blazing suns if she ever wanted a shot at earning her *own* sword.

It seemed impossible.

It seemed like it couldn't be done.

"And now, for our final competitor," Ari called out over the speaker. "She's new to the challenge this year, and she certainly impressed us yesterday in the elimination round. Please give it up for Li!"

The crowd erupted in cheers and shouts and clapping. Lonnie stood and slowly made her way toward the massive structure in front of her. As she walked, it felt as though her legs were made of heavy steel. She had to drag one foot after another. Her mind was screaming for her to go back, turn back, run straight back to Auradon Prep!

You'll fail! a voice inside her head shouted. *You'll never beat him! You're not old enough. Not fast enough. Not strong enough. And then what will everyone think?*

She slowed to a stop, contemplating the words zooming around her mind.

Was the voice inside of her right? Was she foolish to even try when it seemed so undoable? So impossible? So humiliating should she lose?

She searched the crowd for a familiar face, but she couldn't find Jay or Jordan anywhere. That's when she felt the heavy object still tucked inside her jacket. Jordan's genie lamp. And suddenly she remembered what she had told Jordan the previous night when they were trapped in that creepy nightclub.

If you give up now, don't you automatically fail? Isn't trying and failing better than not trying at all?

She'd meant the words for Jordan, but in this moment, staring out into the sea of faces all waiting for her to tackle this final challenge, Lonnie realized those words were meant for her, too. She needed to hear them just as much as Jordan had. All this time, Lonnie had been hiding her true self, afraid of failing in front of everyone. Afraid that if they knew who her mother was, they would judge her more harshly.

But what she'd said to Jordan was true. Trying and failing was better than not trying at all. And even though she'd made it this far in the competition, she hadn't done it as herself. She hadn't done it as Lonnie, daughter of Mulan.

"Is everything all right, Li?" Ari asked over the loudspeaker, clearly urging her to get on with it. She had no idea how long she'd just been standing there, staring into the crowd.

"No!" Lonnie shouted at the top of her lungs, causing everyone in the stands to fall silent.

Lonnie glanced around at her fellow competitors. At the spectators in the stands. At the team of crew and producers from the show who were all gaping at her, wondering what she was going to do next.

"Everything is not all right!" she yelled. She reached up and touched the blond wig on her head. It felt safe. It felt just as protective as the golden warrior's helmet.

But it was time to stop hiding.

It was time to stop being afraid.

Her grip tightened around the wig, and before she

could lose her nerve, she ripped the fake blond hair from her head, shaking out the long, dark locks that were tucked underneath.

"Because I'm not Li," she announced to the entire arena, her voice seeming to echo off the round red walls. "I'm Lonnie, daughter of the great warrior Mulan."

THE BIGGEST CHALLENGE

*I am ready. Win or lose, succeed
or fail, I am going to do this as
myself. And I'm going to deal with
the consequences. Both here in the
arena and back at Auradon Prep,
where everyone is probably watching.*

After the crowd's shocked reaction finally died down, Lonnie took her position on the first wooden plank. The bell chimed, jolting Lonnie into action. She raised her sword as the first blazing sun came zooming toward her. It seemed to move so much faster when she was standing right in front of it than when she was watching from the sidelines. She swung her sword at just the right moment, easily slicing through the fiery ball and sending the shattered, sizzling pieces to the ground.

The next one came just as fast. But it was much higher.

Lonnie scrambled up the wooden planks, fighting to keep her balance as each narrow platform swung under the weight of her steps. She was able to position herself on a plank close to the middle of the structure before turning and carving the air with her sword. The ball burst into tiny pieces of light. The crowd cheered.

For the next forty-five seconds, Lonnie continued to climb and cut, climb and cut, leaping effortlessly and valiantly through the air. She felt good holding that sword. Every time she swung, obliterating another ball of blazing fire, she felt strong and brave and invincible.

Just as she had when she'd battled those pirates alongside the VKs on the Isle of the Lost.

As Lonnie sliced through sun after sun, she seemed to fall into a kind of trance, her intense laser focus taking over her body until she'd almost forgotten where she was. For those forty-five seconds, she wasn't in a giant red dome in the Imperial City, surrounded by thousands of people and watched by tens of thousands more all around the kingdom. She was back in the quiet gardens behind the palace, training with her mother, jabbing and feinting and spinning. The noise of the crowd seemed to disappear until all she could hear was her deep, labored breathing, the whoosh of the sword slicing the air, and the pounding of her own heart.

She had completely lost track of how many suns she had

and pushed off the plummeting plank, wrapping her legs around the rope she was holding to prevent herself from sliding down. Lonnie glided through the air across the structure, hanging on to the rope for dear life with one hand and both legs while her other hand stretched out her sword. She saw the blazing ball sailing past her and she thrust her sword as far as her arm would go, letting out a grunt of effort.

Her sword stabbed straight through the sun, and a glitter of fire rained down around her, sending the audience into a frenzy of raucous applause.

A huge grin spread across Lonnie's face as she turned her head to watch the counter on the wall tick over from twenty-two to twenty-three, just as the clock ran out.

KINDA SWORDA NERVOUS

The competition ended an hour
ago, and here I am, standing in
front of the Imperial Council,
waiting for the real prize.

The eight men and women who made up the Imperial
Council were all incredibly old and dressed in long red silk
robes lined with gold trim. Lonnie felt her heart start to
gallop in her chest.

Why am I so nervous? she asked herself. *If I can take on
the Auradon Warrior Challenge—and win!—I shouldn't be
afraid of anything.*

And yet, she was terrified.

There was something about the council—their serious
expressions, their no-nonsense demeanor, their reputation
for unrivaled wisdom and experience—that unnerved her.

Even though she'd been the youngest person to ever win the Auradon Warrior Challenge, she still felt small and childish staring into their stony faces.

Chen had obviously not been pleased when she'd nabbed the victory. In fact, he'd stormed out of the arena in a huff. And even though Jay had still wanted to go after him and make him pay for trying to sabotage Lonnie, Lonnie had convinced him to let it go.

"I beat him," she'd told Jay calmly. "Isn't that payback enough?"

"No!" Jay had replied, his fists balling at his sides. "I want revenge!"

"Revenge has no honor," Lonnie had explained.

And although it had taken a few minutes for him to calm down, Jay had eventually let the idea sink in. "Honor," he'd repeated with a laugh. "It's not a word you hear a lot on the Isle of the Lost."

"Well," Lonnie had said, "you've come a long way from the Isle of the Lost."

And as Jay had finally agreed to let go of his thirst for revenge, Lonnie hadn't been able to help feeling pride. It had been nice to be able to teach *him* something for a change.

As Lonnie stood in front of the Imperial Council, she realized that though she had come all this way to make her plea for the sword, she had no idea *how* to do it. What should she say? Was she supposed to speak first? Was there a special ceremony she was supposed to perform? The answer came a moment later when one of the members—a man who was seated in the center—spoke. "Lonnie, daughter of Fa Mulan and Li Shang, what is your business here in front of the council?"

Lonnie cleared her throat and tried to make herself look taller. "Hello, members of the council," she said. "Thank you for seeing me. I have come here in regards to the sword of Shan-Yu."

There were quiet murmurs among the council members, and a few of them looked at each other and exchanged confused glances. Finally, the man in the center, clearly their leader, spoke again. "Yes, we received your letter regarding the sword of Shan-Yu, but we were under the assumption that this matter had already been resolved. Did you not receive our reply?"

Lonnie swallowed hard and took a step forward. "I did, your excellencies. And thank you for responding so quickly." She stopped to take a deep breath, trying to steady her still-pounding heart. "In your letter, you said, 'We do not believe you have yet proved your worthiness.'"

"Yes?" the leader replied.

"Well," Lonnie went on after another hard swallow. "I have come here today to tell you that the situation has changed, and I now believe I have proved my worthiness of the sword."

"Oh?" the leader asked. "Is that so?"

Lonnie nodded. "Yes, your excellency. You see, just an hour ago, I was named champion of the Auradon Warrior Challenge." She reached down the front of her uniform and pulled out her medal. "As you probably know, this is the most difficult challenge in all of Auradon."

"We are aware of the competition's complexities," the man replied, somewhat coldly. Then he cracked a rare smile and said, "In fact, we all watched it on TV today."

There were nods of assent across the table.

"Oh!" Lonnie said, feeling somewhat lighter and more relaxed. "Great! So, then, you saw me win?"

"We did," the man replied. "Your feat was quite impressive. It showed great courage and ingenuity."

Lonnie blew out a huge sigh of relief. This was going to be easier than she had expected. "Well, then," she said confidently. "I kindly request that the council reconsider their previous decision to deny me the sword of Shan-Yu, since I have clearly proven my worthiness as a warrior."

The smile instantly vanished from the man's face, and his expression returned to stone. Lonnie felt a squeeze in her chest.

"I am sorry, but that is not possible," said the leader.

Lonnie's jaw dropped. "B-b-but," she stammered. "I won. I beat hundreds of other warriors. I'm now the greatest modern warrior in Auradon. Look! It says so right here!" She hoisted up her medal and pointed at the engraving on the front, which clearly spelled out:

GREATEST MODERN WARRIOR IN AURADON

"Our decision stands," the leader said impassively.

"Aren't you at least going to discuss it with the rest of the council?" Lonnie asked. She could hear the desperation in her voice.

"There is no need. We are unanimous."

Lonnie glanced helplessly from the leader to each of the other seven members. They all gave her tiny, curt nods.

"I don't understand!" Lonnie cried, feeling tears prick her eyes. "There must be some mistake."

"There is no mistake," the leader replied.

Lonnie was suddenly having a hard time catching her breath. This couldn't be happening. This couldn't be real! She'd done everything she was supposed to do. She'd trained all week. She'd gotten to the Imperial City. She'd defeated Chen and survived all his attempts to sabotage her. She'd *won*! How could they possibly turn her down? How could they possibly claim she still wasn't worthy?

Her mind grasped for something else to say. Another argument. Another way to appeal to them. To get them to see they were wrong. She didn't care how ancient and wise they were, they were still *wrong*. There had to be something she could do. Someone else she could talk to. Someone even older and wiser than them.

"The All-Knowing One!" she burst out breathlessly. "I wish to speak to the All-Knowing One!"

That was the answer. Lonnie was sure of it. The All-Knowing One was whom the council reported to. The All-Knowing One was the most respected and revered citizen of the Imperial City.

The leader of the council cocked an eyebrow. "I'm afraid that is impossible. The All-Knowing One does not meet with visitors."

"But—" Lonnie tried to argue, but she was immediately cut off by the leader.

"Congratulations on your victory today, Lonnie, daughter of Fa Mulan and Li Shang. We wish you a safe journey back to Auradon Prep."

The tears were now welling up in Lonnie's eyes, but she did her best to keep them at bay. She didn't want the council to see her cry. They had to think she was brave. They had to think she was worthy. If they saw her blubbering like a baby, they would never, ever grant her request.

But she could see in all their eyes that there was nothing else to say. No more arguments to make. The council was not going to change its mind.

So Lonnie did the only thing there was left to do. She bowed her head in defeat and ran from the room.

SLASHED

I'm pretty much devastated. I cannot believe after all that, after I won the Auradon Warrior Challenge, they still wouldn't let me have my mother's sword.

When Lonnie emerged from the Imperial Palace, Jay was waiting for her on the front steps. He stood up, anxiously peering at her empty hands.

"Wh-wh-where is it?" he fumbled to say, confusion shadowing his features. "What happened?"

All the tears Lonnie had been trying so desperately to hold back slowly started to spill from her eyes. "They said no!"

"*What?*" Jay screeched so loudly that a few palace guards looked over, gripping their swords more tightly. "How could they do that?"

Lonnie sniffled and threw her arms up. "I don't know. They just said I still hadn't proved my worthiness."

Jay was angry now. Lonnie could see it all over his face and in his clenched fists. She was worried he was going to hit something. Like a wall or a post. "But that's total camel crud! You just won the most difficult competition in all of Auradon. You're the new Auradon Warrior! How could they possibly say you aren't worthy?"

The entire way out of the palace, Lonnie had asked herself the same question over and over. But she still hadn't come up with an answer. So she just cried harder. "Let's just go home," she replied. "Let's just go back to Auradon Prep, finish studying for finals, and get on with our lives."

"No!" Jay immediately shot back, startling Lonnie with his intensity. "We're not just going to go home with our tails between our legs. You're not going to let that stupid council intimidate you. And you're not going to take no for an answer." He put his hands on her shoulders and turned her around, back toward the steps. "You're marching right back in there and demanding your sword."

Lonnie shook her head. "It won't work. Their decision is final."

"Then go talk to the All-Glowing One. Didn't you tell me that's who the council reports to?"

Through her tears, Lonnie couldn't help chuckling.

"What?" Jay asked.

"It's the All-*Knowing* One. Not the All-*Glowing* One."

"Whatever!" Jay snapped. "Go find this person and demand your sword. Threaten to kick butt if you don't get it."

Lonnie shook her head. "This isn't the Isle of the Lost. You can't kick the All-Knowing One's butt. That's not how we do things here in Auradon. We respect customs and tradition."

"Well, that's the problem!" Jay argued. "You Auradon kids are too polite. You're too obsessed with the rules and what's 'proper.' If it were me, I would fight back."

"Well," Lonnie said softly, "it's not you, is it? It's me, and I say we're going home."

She walked past him, lightly brushing against his shoulder. She expected Jay to just let it go and follow her back to the suite so they could pack their things, find Jordan, and leave. But he didn't. He continued to stand there with his fists clenched and his breathing heavy. "C'mon, Lonnie," he said after a moment. "Be brave."

Anger coursed through her veins. She spun around. "You have a lot of nerve talking to me about bravery!"

Jay looked taken aback. "Excuse me?"

"If you're so brave," Lonnie challenged, "why don't you just *admit* that you hurt Jordan's feelings and apologize to her instead of putting on this ridiculous charade every time you see her?"

Jay's mouth fell open and he uttered something that sounded more like gibberish than actual words.

"Yeah," Lonnie replied. "I know what happened. Jordan told me. She said that you . . ."

Lonnie's voice trailed off as she realized she didn't actually know what hurtful thing Jay had said to Jordan to make her so mad. Jordan had never gotten around to telling her. She'd started to, but then she had moved to talking about the documentary and how scared she was to finish it, and Lonnie had never heard the rest of the story.

Jay's shoulders slouched. "I said her father's powers were overrated."

Lonnie's eyes widened. "You did what?"

Jay sighed and refused to meet Lonnie's eye. She could tell he was ashamed about what he was about to say. "We were filming Jordan's documentary and, you know, just kind of chatting about stuff. Life, classes, parents. She claimed her father was the most powerful genie of all time, and I . . . well, I didn't agree."

Lonnie narrowed her eyes at him.

"Hey." Jay defended himself, holding up his hands. "I grew up hearing stories about that epic day when my father stole the lamp and enslaved the great and powerful genie. That kind of stuff rubs off on you. Anyway, I was getting annoyed at all the bragging she was doing about her dad, so I casually reminded her of the time her father lost to my father. She totally overreacted, got all huffy, and stormed off."

"And then what?" Lonnie asked.

Jay shrugged, like he didn't understand the question. "And then nothing. She's been mad at me ever since."

"And you haven't apologized?" Lonnie asked, shocked.

Jay scoffed. "No. I don't *apologize*."

"Why not? Are you afraid?" Lonnie challenged him, knowing it was the same thing he'd accused her of being before they'd left Auradon Prep.

"Psh," Jay said, waving this away. "Of course not."

"I think you are. I think you're afraid of admitting you did something wrong. And that's why you've been acting like a total clown around her all weekend. Because you're too cowardly to do the right thing."

Jay opened his mouth to argue, but Lonnie quickly cut him off. "So don't lecture me about bravery. If you were brave, you would just tell her you're sorry. But it looks like bravery is a trait that neither of us really has."

And with that, Lonnie walked away, leaving Jay frozen and speechless on the steps of the Imperial Palace.

She didn't know where she was going. She just knew she had to get away. She had to walk. She had to think. She had to mourn the loss of her precious sword. All alone.

MATCH OVER

I guess there's nothing to do now
but admit defeat. I may have
won the challenge, but I didn't get
what I really came here for.

After wandering around the Imperial City for nearly an hour, Lonnie found herself standing in front of the Hall of Wisdom. She stared up at the majestic structure with its deep red columns and tiered wooden roof.

Her sword was inside those walls.

Not more than a hundred feet from where she stood.

And yet she'd never felt farther away from it.

With a sigh, Lonnie mounted the steps and entered through the heavy wooden doors. She just wanted to look at it. She just wanted to see it one last time before she returned to Auradon Prep.

The great hall was empty of people. The sword of

162

Shan-Yu sat on a gold pedestal in the center of the room, protected by a glass case. Lonnie walked slowly toward it, feeling her disappointment grow with every step. When she reached the pedestal, she pressed her hands against the glass, feeling it shimmer and vibrate beneath her fingers.

She knew from years of coming here as a child to gaze upon her future possession that the glass protecting the sword was enchanted with a special kind of magic. An ancient magic that Lonnie knew nothing about. All she knew was that the glass was unbreakable. Impenetrable. Not even the sharpest sword or the strongest warrior could shatter it.

Lonnie stared at the beautiful weapon behind the glass. The jagged steel sparkled under the lights of the great hall. She let out a long, sorrowful exhale and watched as her breath fogged up the glass and then cleared almost instantly.

"It's just a sword," Lonnie said aloud, trying to make herself feel better. "What's so special about it, anyway?"

So she was going home empty-handed. So what? Even though she hadn't seemed to prove anything to the Imperial Council, she'd certainly proved something to herself. That she was just as mighty and strong and brave as her mother. That she could take on the reigning champion of the Auradon Warrior Challenge and win. That was enough, wasn't it?

The next day she'd simply walk into a shop in downtown

Auradon and purchase a brand-new sword. It would be just as good. It would win her plenty of R.O.A.R. competitions. Sure, it wouldn't be soaked in history like this one. Sure, it wouldn't come with a tradition of honor and bravery. But what did that matter? It would be brand-new, and it would be hers. She didn't need this stupid old sword, anyway.

Lonnie started crying again.

Who was she kidding? Of course she needed this sword! It was her birthright. She was destined to have it.

Just not yet, apparently.

"I don't understand," Lonnie whispered aloud to the weapon held prisoner behind the glass case. "Why can't you be mine? Why won't the council let me have you?"

"Ah, but see, that is where you are mistaken," came a rattling voice from somewhere behind her.

Lonnie gasped and turned around to see a very old woman walking slowly toward her with the help of a cane. The woman's wrinkly skin seemed to fall in layers around the features of her face. She was dressed in a red satin robe, and her snow-white hair was pulled back into a tight bun secured by a black ribbon. It wasn't until Lonnie noticed the necklace of bright green jade hanging around her neck that she realized who this person was.

"The All-Knowing One," Lonnie said, tipping forward into a bow. "I'm sorry. I didn't realize anyone was here."

The old woman ignored her apology and came closer.

"You are mistaken to believe that the council has anything to do with the decision to deny you the sword."

Lonnie's eyebrows knit together in confusion. What was this old lady talking about? "I don't understand," Lonnie said as politely as she could. "It was the council who told me I couldn't have the sword."

The woman smiled, her crinkled eyes brightening. "Yes, but have you ever considered that the council is nothing more than a messenger service, delivering verdicts from another source?"

"You," Lonnie said with sudden realization. "*You* were the one who told them to deny me the sword?"

All this time she'd been blaming the council, when it was *her.* This woman. She was the one responsible for Lonnie's going home empty-handed.

Lonnie wanted to feel anger toward the little old woman who stood before her, but she just couldn't muster any. There was something about the woman's kind, bright eyes that made it impossible to direct any ill will toward her.

"You give me far too much credit, my dear," the All-Knowing One said with a chuckle that sounded more like a croak. "I wouldn't dream of making a decision as important as the destiny of this city's greatest asset." She nodded toward the sword.

Lonnie was confused again. "But if it wasn't you who made the decision, then who did?"

The old woman tilted her head and gave Lonnie a strange look, as though she were surprised Lonnie hadn't yet figured out the answer to her own question. Then she raised her cane and gave the display case a light tap. "Why, it was the sword itself, of course."

Lonnie blinked rapidly, trying to keep up. "The *sword* made the decision?"

"Didn't your mother ever tell you how special this sword was?"

"Well, yes," Lonnie replied. "But she never said it was *magic.*"

The woman's head teetered from side to side. "Magic is a strong word. It's very hard to put a label on something so ancient and steeped in history. Let's just say the sword has been around longer than all of us, and therefore it is quite capable of making its own decisions."

Lonnie closed her eyes tight, trying to wrap her head around everything that was happening. "So you're saying the sword doesn't want me?"

"Oh, no, my dear," the All-Knowing One said, making a *tsk* sound with her teeth. "The sword *knows* it belongs to you. It's just waiting for *you* to prove that you belong to it."

Lonnie felt a scream of frustration rise in her throat. She took a deep breath. "But that's what I did! I proved my worth. I won the Auradon Warrior Challenge. It's the most difficult competition in all the kingdom!"

The woman smiled her crinkly little smile again. "Clearly, the sword is not impressed with such accolades."

"But what more can I do?" Lonnie asked desperately.

The woman leaned forward on her cane. "I suppose there's always the third wish," she whispered.

Lonnie's mouth dropped open in shock. "Y-y-you know about Jordan's lamp?"

"Of course. They don't call me the All-Knowing One for nothing." She cocked her head to the side. "Although I never cared for the title, myself. A bit too flashy for my taste."

"Wait a minute," Lonnie said, holding up her hands. "Are you saying that if I wish for the sword, I'll get it?"

The old woman shrugged. "Genie magic is very powerful."

"But I promised Jordan I would save the third wish for her," Lonnie said, more to herself than to the woman.

The All-Knowing One nodded, as though she, too, could feel the weight of Lonnie's dilemma. "I suppose, then, you must decide how much the sword is worth to you."

It's worth a lot, Lonnie thought immediately.

After all, she had been born to have that sword. She wanted so badly to have it *now*. She wanted to show up at that induction ceremony holding it proudly in her hands. And she did deserve it. She knew that! She didn't care what the All-Knowing One or the council said. She had taken on the hardest challenge of her life and won. She was a warrior. The greatest modern warrior. And she had the medal and cash prize to prove it.

She reached inside the jacket of her uniform and pulled out the lamp. Jordan had given it to her for good luck. And . . .

Just in case you need to use your third wish.

See, a voice inside Lonnie's mind said, *even Jordan wants you to have the sword.*

Jordan was willing to give up her wish for Lonnie's. That's how good of a friend she was. . . .

Lonnie glanced up to see the All-Knowing One studying her closely. "Do you know what you will do?"

Lonnie nodded. "I know what I will do."

ON THE EDGE

I know how this works. I just close my
eyes and rub my hands against the cool
metal surface of the lamp.
And make my final wish.

A strange sound echoed across the large, empty room of the Hall of Wisdom. It sounded like a choir singing and insects buzzing and thunder rolling all at once. Lonnie's eyes shot open, and she jumped back from the golden pedestal.

"What's happening?" she whispered.

Lonnie watched with a mix of fascination and alarm as the glass case around the sword began to shimmer. Like it were made of nothing more than air. The mysterious humming sound grew louder and louder as the clear barrier continued to glisten and sparkle.

"You chose wisely," the All-Knowing One said somewhere behind Lonnie. But Lonnie didn't turn around. She didn't dare peel her eyes away from the magnificent sight that lay in front of her.

Then Lonnie felt a gust of warm air travel through the great hall. She glanced up and swore she saw small specks of gold blowing around her, like very fine glitter. She looked back at the sword and gasped when she noticed that the glass case was no longer there. It had simply *ceased* to exist. The sword was sitting on the pedestal with absolutely no protective case around it.

Certain she must be imagining things, Lonnie slowly extended a trembling hand toward the sword, expecting her fingertips to be blocked. But her hand sailed right through the space where the barrier had once been. She let her fingers graze against the handle of the mighty sword, feeling a tingle soar through her hand, up her arm, and all throughout her body.

"B-b-but," she stammered, bewildered. "There must be some mistake."

"There is no mistake," the All-Knowing One said meaningfully.

Lonnie looked confused. "But I didn't wish for the sword."

She racked her brain, trying to retrace her steps over the past few minutes. There weren't many to retrace. She'd closed her eyes, she'd rubbed the lamp, and deep in her mind, she'd thought the words:

170

I wish for Jordan to be free of her commitment.

She'd kept her promise. She had sworn she would save the final wish for Jordan, and that's exactly what she had done. So then, why was the sword suddenly unprotected? As though it were giving itself to her?

The woman croaked out another laugh. "You see, when you put your own desires aside for the sake of your promise, you not only proved your loyalty to your friend, you also proved your honor. And that is the secret of being a true warrior."

The secret of being a true warrior.

Where had Lonnie heard those words before?

Then the memory came flooding back to her. She saw herself as a little girl, training with her mother under the cherry blossom trees. She'd wanted to keep going, keep practicing, keep fighting, thinking that strength was what proved a person's worthiness. But her mother had smiled that gentle smile of hers and said, *Being a valiant warrior is not about the strength you have here. It's about the strength you have here.* And then her mother had touched Lonnie's chest, right over her heart.

Lonnie hadn't truly understood her mother's words until this very moment. Until she had been faced with the choice that would finally prove her worthiness.

Until the right challenge had presented itself.

Just as her mother had said it would.

"Honor." Lonnie repeated the word aloud, marveling at it just as Jay had done back in the arena. She loved the way it felt on her lips. Like a secret. Like a key that opened any lock. It was more challenging than any obstacle. It was more valued than any medal. And it was something you could never prove with swords or shields or spinning logs.

"The sword of Shan-Yu has seen the honor inside you," the All-Knowing One said, "and it has given itself to you."

Then the old woman stretched out a bony finger and pointed toward the golden pedestal. Toward the glimmering, ancient sword that had waited so patiently for this moment.

Lonnie sucked in a sharp breath and reached out, grasping the sword by its sturdy handle, pulling the mighty weapon toward her.

Claiming her birthright once and for all.

HONOR CONQUERS ALL

Not only did I earn my sword,
but I finally found out what
my mom meant about the
strength in my heart.
I get it now!
Oh, and did I mention I also got
some serious prize money for
winning the challenge?

"You really know how to travel in style!" Jordan exclaimed, leaning back in her blue velvet first-class seat. "A five-star royal suite and now a private car on the high-speed Auradon Express train?"

Lonnie grinned and ran her hands over the sheathed sword in her lap. She hadn't been able to stop touching it.

Since she didn't really have much use for the cash prize that came with winning the Auradon Warrior Challenge,

Lonnie had decided to spend it on train tickets back to Auradon Prep for her and her friends. It was the fastest way to get home, and—in this private first-class car—definitely the most glamorous.

"Pretty nice," Jay said, running his hands over the gold-encrusted fixtures of the compartment.

"Try not to steal anything," Jordan teased.

"Just your heart," Jay quipped back.

"Dream on," Jordan said with a groan.

Lonnie was so happy about having her sword, she didn't even mind that Jay and Jordan were back to their usual squabbling. She glanced down at the mighty weapon in her lap and another huge beaming smile lit up her face.

"You realize we're going to get in a lot of trouble now," Jay said. "After your little de-wigging escapade in the arena, everyone back at Auradon Prep knows you were here. And it won't be long until they figure out Jordan and I were with you."

Lonnie had certainly thought about that. She knew that unveiling herself back in the arena would have consequences, but she didn't care. She was ready to face them. She was ready to face anything. She didn't want to hide anymore.

"That's okay," Lonnie said with a shrug, peering down at her sword again. "Some things are worth getting caught for." Then she glanced between Jay and Jordan and quickly

Lonnie and Jordan both stared at Jay in total shock. Neither could bring themselves to believe the words coming out of Jay's mouth.

"I know I've been acting a little nuts lately," Jay went on, still rushing through his words as though desperate to get them all out. "I think I was just too afraid to admit that I hurt you, so instead I've been trying to cover up the awkwardness by acting silly. Hoping you'd just laugh and forget about being mad. And I'm sorry for that, too."

Jordan was silent for a long time, and for a moment, Lonnie worried that she wasn't going to forgive Jay. That she was going to tell him it was too late for apologies. But then Jordan shook her head and barked out a laugh. "Oh, my gosh, Jay, you are *such* a dork."

Jay looked insulted. "A dork? Seriously? You're calling me a dork?"

Jordan nodded. "I'm calling you a dork."

Jay thought about that for a moment. "A *charming* dork, though, right?"

Jordan pursed her lips thoughtfully. "*Semi*-charming."

"A dork you forgive?" Jay asked, raising an eyebrow.

Jordan cracked a smile. "Of course."

Jay leaned back in his seat, looking proud of himself. Then, a moment later, his smirk turned into a frown. "What did you mean when you said '*semi*-charming'?"

Jordan sighed. "Oh, get over yourself."

"C'mon, admit it, you think I'm just a *little* bit cute."

Jordan shook her head. "Actually, I don't."

"What about my devilish smile?" Jay asked, showing his teeth.

Jordan snorted. "More like *dorkiest* smile."

As the two continued to banter, Lonnie returned her gaze to the window with a contented sigh. Everything was back to normal. In fact, it was better than normal. Because even though she was about to be in deep trouble with Headmistress Fairy Godmother for sneaking out of school, Lonnie was returning with something she hadn't had when she left.

And it was more than just a sword.

FALL ON YOUR SWORD

We're back home now. Gulp.

As the train pulled away from the station, Lonnie, Jordan, and Jay began the short walk to campus. Lonnie knew everyone would probably still be in study mode, locked up in their rooms, trying to cram historical dates and dragon anatomy and fairy compounds into their heads before finals started the next morning.

They crept onto campus, fully expecting Fairy Godmother to be waiting for them in front of the dorms, ready to give them the lecture of a lifetime, but she was nowhere to be seen.

"I'm sure we'll get what's coming to us when she spots us at dinner," Jordan said.

The three parted ways and disappeared into their rooms. When Lonnie got back to her room, she placed the sword of Shan-Yu on her dresser and stood back to admire it. She couldn't believe it was finally hers. It felt too good to be true, but at the same time, it felt right. She deserved that sword. She had earned that sword.

She was *worthy* of that sword.

When dinner rolled around, Lonnie slipped down to the banquet hall and joined Mal, Evie, Freddie, and Ally at one of the tables.

"Haven't seen much of you all weekend," Mal said as soon as Lonnie sat down. "Studying extra hard?"

Lonnie's eyebrows pinched together as she tried to figure out whether or not Mal was joking. How could she not know where Lonnie had been? She had to have seen the competition on TV.

"Um," Lonnie stammered. "Well . . ."

A second later, she felt a hand clamp down on her shoulder, and Lonnie gazed up to see Fairy Godmother looming over her. Her stomach clenched. This was it. She was so busted.

"Hi, Lonnie," Fairy Godmother said, and Lonnie struggled to interpret her tone. Did it sound upset? Disappointed? Furious?

"Hi, Fairy Godmother," she replied warily.

"Are you ready for exams tomorrow?"

Lonnie studied Fairy Godmother's expression, once again trying to figure out if there was a secret meaning behind her words.

"I think so," Lonnie said.

Fairy Godmother flashed a warm smile. It seemed genuine. "Good, good." She then nodded at each of the girls at the table and said, "Well, best of luck to all of you tomorrow!"

Then she shuffled away.

Okay, what is going on? Lonnie wondered.

"Um," Lonnie said again, trying to figure out the best way to broach the subject. "Anyone watch any good TV this weekend?"

Freddie scowled. "We couldn't."

"Couldn't?" Lonnie repeated. "Why? Because of the lock-in?"

"No," Ally replied, looking at Lonnie as though she were out of focus. "Because of the outage. You know that."

"What outage?" Jordan asked, appearing next to the table with a plate of food and sliding into a seat next to Lonnie.

"The Auradon Prep Wi-Fi was out *all* weekend," Evie griped. "Or were you two just so studious you didn't even try to get online?"

"Oh, um," Lonnie faltered. "Right. I forgot." She shared a conspiratorial look with Jordan. "So no one was able to watch *anything* this weekend?" Lonnie confirmed.

"Yeah," Evie replied. "It was sobering."

"So that means Fairy Godmother couldn't watch anything, either?" Jordan asked.

Ally, Mal, Freddie, and Evie exchanged confused glances. "Yeah, exactly. What's going on with you two? Why are you acting so out of it? You were here, too."

"Right," Lonnie said. "We were here, too."

The girls then broke into a conversation about their exams, and Jordan leaned in to whisper to Lonnie. "Your wish!"

"What about it?" Lonnie asked.

"You wished to go to the Imperial City *without getting caught.*"

Lonnie bit her lip. "Are you saying the lamp cut the Wi-Fi so no one here could watch the show?"

Jordan shrugged. "What can I say? Genie magic is pretty awesome."

Lonnie gazed around the bustling banquet hall. Everyone was chatting nervously about finals. No one even seemed to notice they'd been gone.

Lonnie blew out a relieved breath. "It most certainly is."

IT'S A BOUT TIME

Finals? I slew 'em. Now it's time for my official induction into the R.O.A.R. team.

The next night, Lonnie dressed in her warrior uniform and stood in front of the mirror in her dorm room, holding her new sword. She gripped the strong handle and gave the weapon three swift flicks, loving the way it cut through the air.

She stuck her sword into the sheath attached to her belt and made her way downstairs. As she walked to the arena, she spotted Jordan up ahead and ran to catch up with her.

"Are you ready?" Jordan asked.

Lonnie patted her sword. "Absolutely."

"I'm proud of you," Jordan said.

Lonnie grinned. "Me too."

They started to walk the rest of the way together, but just before they reached the arena, someone called out

Jordan's name, and they both turned to see King Ben jogging to catch up to them.

"Hey, Jordan," he said breathlessly. "I wanted to talk to you about that documentary."

Lonnie looked questioningly at Jordan, but Jordan kept her gaze steadily on Ben.

What is this about? Lonnie wondered. *Did my third wish not work?*

"When do you think I can see the final cut?" Ben asked.

Jordan smiled. "I've been working on it all afternoon. I should have something to show you tomorrow morning."

Ben nodded. "Awesome. I'm so excited to see it. I'll find you after breakfast?"

"Perfect," Jordan said.

"See you at the ceremony!" Ben called out, and then jogged ahead of them.

"What was that about?" Lonnie asked after Ben was out of earshot. "I made the wish to get you out of that. Did it not work?"

"No, it did."

"Then why is he asking to see the final cut?"

Jordan's lips curved into a knowing smile. "When we got back last night, Ben found me after dinner and told me I didn't have to do it anymore. But I told him that I wanted to."

Lonnie stopped walking. "You did?"

Jordan laughed and stopped, too. "Don't look so surprised."

"But I thought you were too afraid."

"I was," Jordan said. "Until I saw you reveal yourself in that arena. You took a chance. You faced your fears. And that's when I knew that I had to do the same."

Twenty minutes later, Lonnie stood in the center of the outdoor R.O.A.R. arena, surrounded by her teammates and classmates.

Jay held his own sword high in the air and began the ceremony. "We are gathered here today to officially induct Lonnie as our new R.O.A.R. team captain!"

Everyone around her cheered, and Lonnie's beaming smile grew wider.

"Lonnie has proved to be a worthy opponent, a valiant competitor, and a loyal teammate." Jay flashed her a knowing smirk. "And therefore, it is my *honor* to welcome her to the team."

Jay waited for the thunderous applause to die down before continuing.

"Lonnie," he said in a serious tone, "please present the sword with which you will be inducted as our captain."

Lonnie took one step forward and placed her fingertips on the handle of the weapon attached to her belt. As she did, she felt a strange vibration travel through her. Not quite magic, but something much more than just pride. It was as though everything her mother had done to secure this birthright had seeped right into the sword's tempered steel.

And now, as Lonnie unsheathed the mighty sword of Shan-Yu and held it high above her head, she felt the spirit of the sword reach out and welcome her. Congratulate her. Bind itself to her.

They were connected now. They were a team. And together, they would go on to do great things.